STAR WARS®

BOBA FETT™

A NEW THREAT

ELIZABETH HAND

LUCAS BOOKS

SCHOLASTIC INC.

New York   Toronto   London   Auckland   Sydney
Mexico City   New Delhi   Hong Kong   Buenos Aires

CHAPTER ONE

Tatooine's twin suns hung low above the horizon. Once he had thought they looked like demonic eyes, threatening him.

Warning him.

Daring him.

Now they were almost welcoming.

"Prepare for landing," commanded the youth at the console of *Slave I*. He stared out at the red suns, shadows pooling like blood beneath them. Despite himself, he smiled.

It's good to be back, thought Boba Fett as he leaned into his seat. In the cockpit behind him was a pair of shriveled hands — all that remained of Boba's last mission. He had gone to the Dune Sea to hunt down the Noghri assassin Jhordvar. The lithe, lidless-eyed alien had made the mistake of betraying Boba's employer.

Bad idea, Boba thought, recalling Jhordvar's contempt when he first peered from his desert hideout to see the young bounty hunter standing before him.

"Jabba sends a lackey to do an assassin's job!" the alien hissed.

"Wrong," said Boba. His blaster was already aligned with Jhordvar's eyes. "He sent the best bounty hunter of his house."

Their battle had been brief but intense. Boba offered Jhordvar the chance to accompany him back to Jabba's B'omarr citadel, but the alien refused to surrender.

Jabba the Hutt had wanted the traitor dead or alive. *Well, he got one out of two*, Boba thought as he guided *Slave I* into the docking bay of Jabba's palace. A desert sandstorm had stranded him for several days in the Noghri's lair, with the alien's body caught outside in the storm. Sand and heat had mummified what remained of Jhordvar. The hands had literally been snapped off by the fierce winds; Boba decided that Jhordvar's ring would be enough to identify him, and so he left the body but took the hands.

"You know, Jhordvar, you should've surrendered when you had the chance," said Boba as *Slave I* touched down. "But you fought bravely, I'll give you that." Boba commanded the ship's computer to shut down, then picked up the Noghri's withered claws. He looked at them, grimacing, then slung them into his pack and disembarked. He left his Mandalorian helmet in the cockpit — he'd get it after he reported in to Jabba.

"I'll see you again soon," he said, letting his hand slide along *Slave I*'s hull. "Real soon."

A pair of Gamorrean guards lolled by the entrance to Jabba's castle. As Boba approached, one of them nudged the other. The two looked at each other in surprise, but quickly straightened.

One of them grunted questioningly.

"I had a slight delay," retorted Boba. He shifted his pack so the hulking boars could get a glimpse of Jhordvar's claws protruding from the top. "Nothing serious. Just a sandstorm."

The Gamorrean guards' eyes widened with respect and — yes! — fear. Boba fought the urge to grin triumphantly. That was almost all the reward he needed. Almost — but not quite. He tipped his head back and stared pointedly at one of the Gamorreans. Hastily the guard turned and opened the massive door for him. Boba strode through proudly.

He would take all the respect he could get. *One earns respect*, his father had always told him. *As for those who are foolish enough not to give it to you — well, for them, there is always fear.*

Boba paused. The heavy door behind him slammed shut. He blinked, waiting for his eyes to adjust to the dimness inside the fortress. He waited for his skin to adjust to the touch of cool air, and for his ears to catch the distant sounds of revelry from the throne room.

Fear and respect, he thought with grim satisfaction. *Everything I've learned about those things can be summed up in three little words:*

Jabba the Hutt.

Boba turned, and began walking down the corridor. Several protocol droids hurried past him, on their way to do Jabba's bidding. Two of the Huttese crimelord's Drovion security guards swaggered up and down the halls. Boba watched as they stopped a pair of Jawas, frisking the small yellow-eyed scavengers before letting them pass. As Boba approached, he had the satisfaction of hearing one of Jabba's lackeys mutter his name.

"G'wan," the Drovion spat, waving him past. "You're expected. As a matter of fact, you're early — no one thought you'd be back this soon."

"Some hoped you wouldn't make it back at all!" his companion laughed.

Boba gave him a cold look. "I'll be sure to mention that to Jabba."

The lackey cringed as Boba went on. Being

Jabba's favored bounty hunter definitely had its advantages.

When he reached the passage leading to the throne room, he stopped. He could see a dozen or so shadowy figures milling inside the corridor. He recognized several of them by their weapons and body armor: bounty hunters.

Something's going on, thought Boba. *But what?*

From inside, shrill music and harsh laughter echoed — the usual sounds of depravity that surrounded Jabba the Hutt.

There was another sound, too, almost as loud.

Boba's stomach was growling.

I haven't eaten since yesterday afternoon, he thought. *And it's going to take a while to tell Jabba the whole story about Jhakva. Plus, this will give me a chance to hear any gossip about what's happened since I left. . . .*

He glanced back toward the throne room. Besides the bounty hunters, he saw droids and several ragged-looking space pirates, a young Twi'lek dancer twitching from nerves, and an Arkanian holding a very young and very active Arkanian dragon on a leash.

Looks like Jabba might be distracted for a few more minutes, Boba figured. Quickly he turned and hurried down a side passage.

"At last! You've come with the new worm cast-ings!" A Selonian wearing a white chef's robe over its sleek-furred body peered out from a doorway. When it saw Boba, its face fell.

"My mistake," it said, and turned back to stir-ring something disgusting in a bubbling pot.

Boba kept moving. He passed several door-ways, each with a sign on it in Huttese characters. KITCHEN FOUR, KITCHEN FIVE, KITCHEN SIX . . .

"Kitchen Seven," said Boba with relief as he came to the last door. He adjusted his pack and went inside.

Immediately, he was greeted by the warm sim-mering scents of baking pod-bread, yowvetch cus-tard, scry-mint. A gnarled figure was bent over a steaming oven. Beside him, another figure was put-ting the finishing touches on a white worm soufflé.

"Am I too late for breakfast?" asked Boba.

"No breakfast till tomorrow," the elderly figure said without looking up.

"Not even for a starving bounty hunter?"

The two cooks turned.

"Boba!" cried the younger one. She swiped the hair from her eyes, leaving a smudge of flour. "You're back! And you've gotten even taller!"

Boba grinned. "Maybe you're just shrinking, Ygabba."

Ygabba shook her head. She looked him up and down. "Nope. You're definitely taller. You're going to need some new body armor soon, Boba."

Boba took the pack from his shoulders and set it on the floor. "Tell me about it," he said. "That'll be my first order of business with Jabba. Second, actually." He cocked a thumb at what was in the pack.

Gab'borah looked down. He was Ygabba's father. As Jabba's head dessert-chef, he was accustomed to seeing all kinds of revolting things.

But even he was impressed by Boba's trophy.

"Jabba will be very pleased," Gab'borah said. He poked at one of the withered hands approvingly. "I didn't even recognize your voice, Boba. And Ygabba's right — you've grown."

The old man smiled and pointed to the wall behind Boba. There, over the past two years, Gab'borah had lined up Ygabba and Boba, drawing a line where the top of their heads met the wall. Boba looked at the most recent mark, and, yes, he was many centimeters taller now.

"Bounty hunting must agree with you," said Gab'borah with a wink. He turned and took a plate of yowvetch custard, still warm and quivering from the oven. "Here, Boba — you look half-famished."

Boba began eating ravenously. "Mmmm — this is great," he said.

"Don't take too long with it," Ygabba warned. "Something's happening. There's a bunch of bounty hunters who've been waiting for the last three days to see Jabba. He's been putting them off — I think he was hoping you'd return — but I don't think he's going to wait much longer."

"Mmmmff." Boba swallowed the last bit of custard, wiping his mouth on his sleeve. "Thanks, Ygabba. And Gab'borah. For the food, and the news." He grabbed his pack and headed back into the hall. Ygabba grinned and waved after him.

"See you, Boba!"

"Make sure you drop by before you leave again," Gab'borah called as Boba strode back toward the throne room. "You'll need more provisions to fill that new body armor!"

This time, Jabba's hangers-on made a point of moving out of the way as soon as they saw Boba coming. He caught the sideways, suspicious looks the other bounty hunters gave him as he passed.

Yet he also saw them gazing at him with grudging admiration — especially when they saw the pair of mummified hands sticking out of his pack. When he reached the entrance to the throne room, he stopped. A short distance away, he could see Jabba's huge form, rising from clouds of incense and smoke like a mountain of sand from the Dune

Sea. Even now Boba could not help grimacing at the sight of his employer.

Man, that is one gross Hutt, he thought. He gestured at a protocol droid standing nearby.

"You," commanded Boba. The droid swiveled, fixing him with its glowing lidless eyes. "Tell Jabba the Hutt that Boba Fett is here."

The droid inclined its gleaming head slightly.

"Yes, sir," it intoned, and walked smoothly into the throne room, past the guards. The waiting bounty hunters watched as the droid approached the throne, then cried out in its clear robotic voice.

"Lord Jabba! My Lord —"

Heads turned and the music grew still as Boba strode into the room. The droid turned and bowed.

"As you can see, O Mighty Jabba — Boba Fett has returned!"

CHAPTER TWO

"Hoh hoh hoh!"

Boba stiffened as familiar deep laughter thundered through the vast room. On a platform in the center of the hall reclined the huge, sluglike form of Jabba the Hutt. Behind him, Jabba's Twi'lek majordomo, Bib Fortuna, stood at attention.

The notorious gangster's yellow eyes fixed themselves on Boba. As the young bounty hunter strode closer to the throne, the great Hutt raised himself to gaze down on him.

"So!" boomed Jabba in Huttese, a language that Boba now knew well. "The prodigal hunter has returned!" The crime lord's eyes narrowed as he stared fixedly at Boba. "But he has returned alone. I see no sign of Jhordvar!"

"That's because the boy has failed!" hissed a voice from the shadows. Boba glanced aside. He saw another bounty hunter, a bulbous-eyed, snoutnosed Aqualish, staring at him hungrily.

"Failed?" Jabba reached for a basket of squirming white worms. He grabbed a fistful of the repellent grubs. "Is this so?"

Boba shot a cold look at the gloating Aqualish. "It is not, O Most Heinous of Hutts," Boba said. He swung his pack from his shoulder and stepped toward the throne. "I did as you commanded, Lord Jabba. I gave the assassin Jhordvar the choice of returning with me, or —"

"Or getting away!" cried the Aqualish.

Rough laughter came from the other bounty hunters. Boba ignored them.

"Or accepting his own death," Boba continued cooly. "He chose the latter. Unfortunately for him. But not, O Mighty Jabba, for you."

With a flourish, Boba lifted his pack and turned it over. Jhordvar's remains fell to the floor. The withered hands curled upward, as though trying — too late — to escape. Gasps echoed through the throne room, followed by excited murmurs.

Jabba looked at his major-domo.

With a bow, Bib Fortuna moved quickly toward the trophies. He stooped and grasped one skeletal hand. Then he turned it so that Jabba could see the gold-green amaralite ring glittering on a mummified finger.

"It is indeed Jhordvar," said Bib Fortuna. He

flashed Boba an admiring look. Then the Twi'lek yanked the ring from the assassin's bony hand, and returned to hold it up to Jabba.

"Hmmmm," mused Jabba. He had Fortuna hold the ring up to the light and inspected it. He looked at Boba. Very slowly, Jabba's lipless mouth parted in a smile. "Hoh hoh hoh! Come —"

Boba let his breath out in a silent whistle of relief. He took the steps toward Jabba at a near run, stopping before the throne.

"Your hand," commanded Jabba. Boba extended his palm, and Jabba dropped the ring into it. "You will receive your usual fee, young Fett. This is a bonus. Amaralite is worth much in some parts of the galaxy."

But not on Tatooine, brooded Boba, while making sure he only looked back calmly at his employer.

"Thank you, Lord Jabba," he said. "I will take good care of it."

Jabba stared at him as though he could read the young man's thoughts. The Hutt's flaccid tongue flicked at the corner of his mouth as he reached for more grubs. "You may find it useful, young Boba," he boomed. "On your next adventure . . ."

Boba stared at him, trying not to let his confusion show. In the hall behind him he could hear the assembled bounty hunters whispering angrily among themselves.

"My next . . . ?" he started.

"Yes." Jabba gestured disdainfully at the other hunters. "You see them? Jackals! Arrak snakes! They are predators. They are good hunters — but they are not great ones. They lack vision. They lack endurance," his voice boomed. "They lack the will to succeed."

Boba allowed himself a small, grim smile. "Endurance I can understand," he said.

"I know," said Jabba. "That is why I have waited for your return. I have an important job for you. It will take many bounty hunters — but only one will be given the most rewarding task."

"This I understand, too," said Boba.

"These bounty hunters," Jabba went on, pointing at the others, "they have been here for a week. Some did not have the patience to wait. They left. They will not return."

Boba shivered at Jabba's tone. The crime lord's voice rose as he cried out so that all in the hall could hear him. "Return in one hour! You will receive your orders then. There will be glory for all of you — and blood for all," he finished, his wide mouth curling in a smile. Throughout the cavernous room, the other bounty hunters cursed. Some laughed. The rest made threatening gestures and stalked away angrily.

After a few minutes only a few remained, looking hopefully at Jabba. One of them was the Aqualish.

"What are you waiting for?" Jabba bellowed at them. He turned to Bib Fortuna. "These guests do not know their manners! Perhaps they would enjoy sharing a meal with my pit beasts?"

"By all means, master," said the Twi'lek with a nasty smile.

Boba looked over. The remaining bounty hunters hurried toward the arched doorway. The last to leave was the Aqualish. He glared back at Boba, then followed the others.

"Now," thundered Jabba from his throne. He leaned forward, his tail twitching slightly, and beckoned Boba toward him. "You have done well for a young bounty hunter."

"Thank you, Lord Jabba," said Boba.

"So well, in fact, that I have no more use for you here," Jabba continued.

Boba looked at him, startled. "But you just said . . . ?" he asked. "No more use for me?"

He swallowed, trying not to let his alarm show.

But all I want is to be a bounty hunter, he thought. *The very best — and only the very best work for Jabba!*

"That is not what I said." Jabba's voice was calm, with an edge of menace. "I said I had no more use for you *here*, on Tatooine."

Boba stared at him, hardly daring to believe his ears.

Jabba nodded. "That is right. Tomorrow you begin a new job for me, Boba — off-planet!"

CHAPTER THREE

Off-planet! Yes!

Boba wanted to punch the air in excitement.

"When do I leave?" he asked.

Jabba watched him approvingly. "I am glad to see you are pleased at the prospect," he boomed. He picked up a squishy, star-shaped glubex, unpeeled its head from its body, and ate it, slurping loudly. He held out the empty skin to Boba.

"Uh, no thanks," said Boba.

Jabba belched and went on. "Many would be terrified at the very thought of traveling to Xagobah in these troubled times. But I think my instincts about you are correct. You do not seem afraid."

Boba hesitated. "My father taught me that fear can be overcome," he said at last. He felt a pang at the memory of his father, Jango Fett — the mighty bounty hunter, slain by that murderous Jedi, Mace Windu. "He always said that a good bounty hunter ought to know his prey as well as he knew himself.

Knowledge is power. Fear is energy. And with power and energy, one can conquer anything. One can defeat any enemy."

Jabba stared at him through slitted amber eyes. "Your father taught you well, Boba Fett."

"What he did not teach me, O Jabba, I have learned from you."

Jabba's enormous mouth opened in a bubbling laugh. He reached for the withered stalk of Jhordvar's arm and waved it as though it were a fan. "Hoh hoh! In that case, you have learned well indeed!"

Jabba tossed Jhordvar's arm into the shadows. "But you will need all your knowledge, young Fett," he said. "And luck wouldn't hurt — not where I'm sending you."

Boba waited patiently. He knew better than to interrupt Jabba.

At this point, Jabba's major-domo took over. "Last week a high-ranking member of the Republic Senate contacted the great Jabba. Completely confidential, of course," the obsequious Bib Fortuna said with an evil smirk. "They want it to appear that they are working through the proper channels. They have put a bounty on the heads of many leading Separatists. Our Lord Jabba had agreed to help them hunt down these scum. Everyone knows his bounty hunters are the best," Bib Fortuna added, gloating. "Even the Republic!"

Boba smiled. His hand moved instinctively to the blaster nestled at his hip. "So you want me to hunt them down?"

"No." The Twiilek gestured dismissively at the empty hall. "Lord Jabba will let those others do that."

Boba glanced at Jabba. The crime lord was watching him closely. Boba kept his expression calm. He waited as Fortuna continued. "Jabba has something much more hazardous in mind for you."

Boba nodded. "Great!"

"Have you ever heard of a Separatist named Wat Tambor?"

"No," said Boba.

"He is the Separatists' Techno Union Foreman, as well as a combat engineer. A brilliant strategist. And extremely dangerous — an expert at fighting machines, and a master of defense technologies. He is also an expert at escape. The Republic captured and detained him at a high-security facility. But several of Tambor's followers from the Techno Union freed him, with the assistance of a Clawdite shapeshifter."

"A Clawdite," repeated Boba, scowling. "I have grown to hate Clawdites."

He didn't say why — namely that a young shape-shifter had robbed him while Boba was on Aargau, trying to regain his father's fortune.

"Lord Jabba's sources inform him that Wat Tambor is now on Xagobah," said Bib Fortuna. "He has taken refuge in his fortress there. Republic troops have laid siege to his hideout, using a clone army led by a Jedi Master named Glynn-Beti."

At the word "Jedi," Boba's face grew grim. He didn't explain that he had actually met Glynn-Beti, back on the assault ship *Candaserri.* She had even shown kindness to him; she had never learned his real name or parentage. Glynn-Beti was a Bothan, cream-furred and small — less than a meter and a half in height. But she had great presence and command despite her diminutive size — the power and authority of a Jedi.

And nothing could change Boba's mind about that.

He said, "I hate the Jedi, too."

But not Ulu Ulix, Glynn-Beti's Padawan, Boba thought. Ulu was the one Padawan he genuinely liked.

Jabba nodded. Fortuna continued, "I know. And the Separatists supporting Wat Tambor have assembled a huge counterforce — hailfires, spider droids, the most technologically advanced battle droids anyone has ever seen. To reach Wat Tambor you will first have to get through Republic and Separatist lines — no member of the Republic forces on Xagobah must know you have this assignment."

"I understand," said Boba.

"Do you?" Jabba's mouth suddenly split into a cold smile.

Fortuna resumed speaking. "Once you have breached the Separatists' forces — if you can — you still have to enter the Citadel. Wat Tambor designed it himself. He focused all of his technological knowledge to one end: to make that fortress invincible. No one has ever penetrated its defenses. No one — not even a Jedi. And even if they did, inside, there are traps everywhere. Hidden doors. And there's a rumor that Tambor is protected by something more terrible still!"

Jabba leaned forward. His huge girth shifted on his throne, like a mud slide in slow motion. "You saw those other bounty hunters, Boba. Every one of them wanted this job. Some of them would be willing to kill for it! Are you?"

CHAPTER FOUR

"When do I leave?" asked Boba. He tried not to look impatient.

"Almost immediately."

Jabba turned and spoke to Fortuna in a low voice. The Twi'lek listened, glancing at Boba, then gave a nod, bowed, and left.

"I have commanded that your ship be refueled and supplied," said Jabba. "The other hunters have already received their assignments from Bib Fortuna. They will be departing soon as well. But only you will be going to Xagobah."

Jabba reached into a vivarium. He plucked a single wuorl from the mass of froglike creatures squirming inside the tank, plopped it into his mouth, and chewed thoughtfully.

Ugh! thought Boba. He quickly looked down, adjusted the relay on his blaster, and waited for Jabba to finish.

"There is a small matter we still need to dis-

21

cuss," Jabba said. He gave another hearty belch. "Your fee."

"My fee?" Boba pretended to mull this over.

He knew he must choose his words very carefully. He did not want to appear too anxious, like those other bounty hunters. He must be clever, and sly. Even more clever than Jabba himself — only Jabba must never know that.

"It is a very difficult bounty," Boba said at last. "The most perilous I have ever heard of. I have been working for you for several years now, O Most Humongous of Hutts. You, more than anyone, know how loyal I am to you. And how grateful I am that you have considered me for this task, knowing that I am still young."

Boba lowered his head. His voice was respectful; but not even Jabba the Hutt could see the determined look in the young bounty hunter's eyes. "Lord Jabba! I will accept whatever fee you feel is appropriate."

Jabba's vast body seemed to balloon with delight. "Once again, a good answer! You alone show appreciation for my care! You alone I can always depend on. Therefore I will split the fee the Republic has promised me. I will keep seventy percent. The rest is yours, Boba."

Only thirty percent! Others might laugh, or argue,

but Boba knew better than that — Jabba usually kept ninety percent.

Boba bowed. "Thank you, Most Generous of Gangsters. As you say, I am still young, and learning. And when I return from this mission, I will continue to work for you. By then my apprenticeship will be over. My fee will be higher. But my loyalty will remain the same."

Boba's heart beat fast as he spoke these last words. He was taking a chance, and he knew it.

But being the best bounty hunter in the galaxy was all about chance. He stared unflinching at Jabba and waited for his reply.

For a moment Jabba was silent. His yellow eyes blazed.

"When you return? *When you return?*" he said at last. His body began to shake with laughter. "Hoh hoh! Don't you mean *if* you return?" Jabba drew back upon his throne. "Go — now! Ready yourself for your adventure! *If* you return, we will discuss this further!"

"Yes, Lord Jabba," Boba replied. With a small bow he turned and very quickly left the throne room.

That was a close one! he thought.

Jabba's tone and the angry look in his eyes told Boba that he had gone perhaps too far this time!

Boba went to his quarters, a small set of rooms

in the easternmost tower of Jabba's sprawling palace. When he got there, he hesitated and stood before the door.

It had been several months since he had been back. He was never here for more than a few days or weeks at a time, between jobs. Still, these rooms were the closest thing he had to a home.

He knew what he would find inside. His quarters were simple, almost spartan. The rooms of a warrior, with no frills besides a small stack of holobooks at his bedside. Books on strategy, navigation, Mandalorian weaponry techniques, scouting, and hunting; ancient texts on war.

Most precious of all was the book left to him by his father. It contained his father's words and images. Along with his father's helmet, and the remnants of his father's armor, the book was Boba's most prized possession. He had learned more from that book than he had from any other.

But he had learned even more from his own experience.

Thinking about his father still made Boba sad. But he knew his father would be proud of his son. After all, he had just received a prize assignment from Jabba the Hutt!

Boba opened the door and went inside. His room was exactly as he had left it. Or was it?

"Hey . . ." Boba frowned.

Hadn't he left his Mandalorian helmet on board *Slave I*?

Yet here it was, in the middle of his bed. Boba glanced around the room suspiciously.

But there was no sign of anyone. The door showed no signs of forced entry. His hand hovering above his blaster, he crossed to the bed.

There was something else there, next to his father's helmet.

A set of armor.

At first he thought it was the body armor that had belonged to Jango — armor that Boba had longed to wear, but which was still too big for him.

"Huh," he said. He picked up the chest-piece, molded to fit Jango's muscular frame. "Wait a minute — something's different."

The body armor was smaller than his father's. Boba held it up — and yes, it was sized to fit him. Perfectly.

He examined the armor carefully, still frowning.

"Wow," he breathed in amazement.

There, slightly below the left side of the rib cage, a small indentation showed where long ago Jango had barely survived an assassin's blast.

Boba whooped in delight.

It was Jango's body armor!

"This is great!" he exclaimed aloud. Quickly he shut and locked his door. Then he changed from his customary uniform — a young Mandalorian soldier's pale blue tunic and trousers, the black knee-high boots that had been too small for him for almost a year. "I hope this fits!"

It did — as if it had been made just for him. Blue fire-resistant pants with steel-colored armored kneepads and shinpads. An adult's tunic, much heavier and more durable than a youth's, with shoulder and chest armor, heavy weapons belt, wrist holsters, and protective gloves that felt like a second, sleeker skin. Last of all, Boba pulled on the boots — his father's boots, but with newly reinforced soles and heels that could withstand temperatures hot enough to melt iron. He had just grabbed his helmet when there was a knock at the door.

"Boba?" asked a familiar voice. "It's me, Ygabba —"

"And me, Gab'borah," chimed in a second voice. "Can we come in?"

"Sure!"

Boba yanked the door open. In the hall stood Ygabba and Gab'borah. Both of them were grinning ear to ear.

"It fits!" cried Ygabba. "I knew it would!"

Boba stared at her. "You did this?"

"Yes! With his help." She cocked a thumb at her father. "Why do you think we were so careful to get your height measurement last time you were here? We knew you'd grow from that — and it looks like we were right!"

Boba shook his head. He looked down at his new body armor, then at Ygabba and Gab'borah.

"This is the best thing anyone has ever given me," he said. He held up his helmet. "Except for this. And this —"

He reached for his father's book, carefully slipped it into a pocket. "Ygabba. Gab'borah. How can I ever thank you?"

Gab'borah shook his head. "You saved my daughter from that horrible Neimoidian, Gilramos," he said. "I will forever be in your debt."

"And don't forget — you saved all those other kids, too, Boba," said Ygabba. She looked at him, then pointed to his helmet, grinning. "I hope you didn't mind me picking that up for you from *Slave I*. I thought you'd want to try it on with the rest of your body armor. And you know, it wasn't the first time I've held on to that helmet for you."

Boba laughed. When he first met Ygabba, she had been a street urchin, forced to steal for the evil Gilramos Libkath. And one of the things she'd tried to steal was his helmet!

"It sure wasn't," he said. "But it might be the last. Jabba is sending me on another bounty hunt."

"So soon?" said Gab'borah.

Boba nodded. "Yeah. But this is the great thing — it's my first job off-planet!"

"Awesome!" said Ygabba. Her voice held a touch of envy. "Where?"

Boba hesitated. More than anything, he wanted to tell them of his prize assignment. After all, Gab'borah and Ygabba were the closest thing Boba had to a family.

But he could not afford the risk. He was in the first rank of Jabba's bounty hunters now.

And he wanted to stay there.

"I can't tell you," he said. "It would be too risky. Not just for me, but for you, too."

Ygabba looked disappointed, but her father nodded.

"We understand," he said. His voice sounded wistful, but his blue eyes shone. "We are very proud of you, Boba. Your father would be proud, too."

Gab'borah reached into the pocket of his chef's robe and withdrew a small packet. "Here. These will last a long time. Wherever you're going, you'll need food." Boba took the packet. He peeled back a corner to see what was inside.

"Gleb rations!" He made a face, then said, "I

mean, thank you, Gab'borah." Gleb rations didn't taste very good, but a single small cube provided enough energy and nutrients for a day's hard work.

"We'd better go," said Ygabba. She gave Boba a wistful smile. "I have one more thing for you. Not as exciting as gleb rations, but . . ."

She held out a small object, about the size of Boba's hand.

"What is it?" he asked, taking the object. It was heaver than it looked, encased in a gray plasteel container.

"A surprise," said Ygabba. "Wait till you get wherever it is you're going. Then open it."

Boba nodded. "Thanks, Ygabba."

"You're welcome. I hope it helps." She grinned at Boba, pointing at his helmet. "You take care of that, too. I won't be around to watch it for you!"

Boba smiled. "Don't worry, " he said, waving good-bye as the two of them turned and walked back down the hall. "I will."

CHAPTER FIVE

Boba had been off-planet before, of course.

He had been born on rainswept Kamino, and had buried his father on Geonosis, a desert planet even more desolate than Tatooine. He had been to Aargau, where he retrieved what remained of his father's fortune and explored the planet's treacherous, mazelike Undercity. And before that he had been on a moon of Bogden, and the poisoned world of Raxus Prime. Raxus Prime was where Boba had met up with the man his father had called "The Count."

Some people knew the Count as Dooku, a leader of the Separatists. Others knew him as Tyranus. Darth Tyranus was the agent who had chosen Jango Fett as the source for the Republic's vast clone army.

Now the Republic and the Separatists were at war. Count Dooku and Tyranus were on opposing sides of the conflict.

And only Boba Fett knew that Tyranus and Dooku were the same man.

This knowledge had saved Boba's life on Aargau. This knowledge was a weapon.

Like a weapon, it gave Boba great power.

And like a weapon, it had the power to kill those who used it.

In the cockpit of *Slave I*, Boba made a last-minute check that his firearms were stored and ready for use.

"Jet pack, blaster, jet pack generator, ion stunner, grappling missile . . ." Boba counted off his deadly array. "Dart shooter, rocket launchers, whipcord thrower . . ."

Jabba might be greedy and disgusting and power-hungry. But when it came to outfitting his favorite bounty hunter, he was as generous as his Gamorrean guards were stupid.

New weapons gleamed from *Slave I*'s storage bays: blaster, ionizers, plasma missiles. And, at Boba's request, Jabba had arranged for brand-new sensor-jammers to be installed on *Slave I*, as well as a state-of-the-art interstitial stealth shield. But best of all was the shining set of Westar-34 blasters on Boba's weapons belt.

"I'll never let you down, Father. Not as long as I

have these," Boba murmured as he checked a blaster's power cell cartridge.

Once the Westar-34s had belonged to Jango Fett. Now they were his son's. The blasters had been designed by Jango, and specially made for him. Compact enough to fit in a jet pack, the weapons were cast of a nearly priceless dallorian alloy, designed to withstand furnace heat.

Boba wasn't sure what was in store for him on Xagobah. But he was pretty sure things would heat up once he got there.

He settled behind the ship's console and set his course for Xagobah. He glanced out the viewscreen.

"Looks like I'm not the only bounty hunter anxious to leave," he said.

In the docking bay around him, dozens of other ships were getting ready to depart Tatooine. Astromech droids and Ughnaught mechanics were everywhere, scrambling to make last-minute adjustments to starships and speeders. In the hazy, red-tinged air above him Boba could make out more starships, flashing like falling stars. He pressed *Slave I*'s thruster igniters.

With a deafening rumble and an explosive burst of flame from its fusion reactors, *Slave I* shot from the landing bay.

"Yes!"

Boba's heart pounded with the thrill that accompanied every new mission. Below him, the Dune Sea spread like flame across the surface of Tatooine. And like flame the brilliant red-and-orange dunes almost immediately faded into black, as *Slave I* pierced the planet's atmosphere and headed into the vast realm of space.

Boba checked the coordinates for Xagobah. He glanced out the viewscreen and saw the usual flash and flare of planets and distant stars.

He frowned. "What's that?"

At the bottom of the viewscreen, something glittered and darted like an asteroid. Something that shouldn't be there.

"There's no asteroids in this sector," said Boba. "No recent planetary upheavals . . ."

Boba quickly checked *Slave I*'s flight plan. There was no sign of meteor activity. The glittering spark grew larger on the viewscreen. Boba leaned forward.

"That's no meteor!"

Instinctively he reached for the control unit of *Slave I*'s missile deployer.

"That's a fighter!" he cried. "And it's tailing me!"

His fingers flashed across the console. Immediately the enlarged image of a Koro-1 exodrive airspeeder filled the screen. Furiously Boba punched at the console. He needed that vehicle's registration data . . .

Silvery letters filled the screen. *Andoan registry, licensed to Urzan Krag of Krag Fanodo.*

"The Aqualish," Boba breathed. "He wanted this assignment, too. Well, he's not going to get it!"

Before him on the viewscreen was a white-hot burst. *Slave I* shuddered as though it were starting re-entry.

"He's firing on me!"

Immediately Boba went into attack mode. The Andoan vessel blinked from sight.

"He has a cloaking device," muttered Boba. "Well, so do I."

Boba deployed *Slave I*'s sensor jammers, then activated the protose detectors. They indicated that the Andoan ship was somewhere behind him.

"You want to play hide-and-seek?" said Boba. He grasped the controls of *Slave I*'s laser cannons and fired. "Well, hide from *that*!"

The energy bolts streaked through the black emptiness outside the ship. They found their target and seemed to liquefy around it. The Andoan speeder's outlines appeared, cloaked in a blazing plasma skin.

The Andoan vessel seemed to hover like a teardrop waiting to fall.

An instant later a blinding flare of blue-white plasma engulfed the Aqualish's ship.

"Gotcha!" exclaimed Boba.

Backlash waves of energy from the blast pulsed around *Slave I*, then dispersed. Where the Andoan speeder had been, brilliant specks of debris floated, like a miniature asteroid field.

"What a great way to start the day!" gloated Boba. His eyes shone as he activated *Slave I*'s navigation program. He leaned forward, his fingers automatically programming the coordinates for his destination.

"Next stop — Xagobah!"

CHAPTER SIX

Boba was not surprised that Wat Tambor had chosen Xagobah for his citadel. This entire sector was known to be a favorite of smugglers making their way between more habitable regions. Jabba had underworld contacts on various planets there.

Still, until he had received his assignment, Boba had never heard the crime lord mention Xagobah.

He had never heard *anyone* mention it.

"But there it is," he murmured.

Dead ahead of *Slave I*, a planet shimmered into view. Boba blinked, wondering if his eyes had gone funny.

The planet seemed out of focus. Its outlines were blurred, as though a vast hand had drawn it with colored ink, then smudged it.

Yet as *Slave I* drew nearer, Boba saw that the problem was not with his eyes. The problem was with Xagobah.

The entire planet seethed with colors. Purple, violet, lavender, maroon, plum: every shade of purple Boba had ever seen, and many he could not have imagined. The colors shifted and moved above the world's surface like an immense, restless demonsquid. Tentacles of indigo and violet spiked thousands of kilometers upward into the atmosphere, then retracted. As *Slave I* began its descent, Boba glimpsed jagged flashes of lightning below Xagobah's violet haze.

Atmospheric storms.

"That's not good," he said to himself.

He saw something else, too. It hovered hawk-like, safely out of reach of the lightning storms — one of the largest vehicles he had ever seen.

A Republic assault ship.

"They sure mean business," Boba said grimly. Quickly he checked to make sure *Slave I*'s cloaking device was still activated. "Now — let's take a closer look."

He drew *Slave I* as close as he dared to the troopship. It was an Acclamator, one of the military transports specially built by the Republic to carry clone troops across the galaxy. Each ship held up to 16,000 clone troopers, as well as armored walkers, gunships, speeders, and ammunition supplies.

And there would be Republic command person-

nel on board as well — and Republic military com-
manders on Xagobah's surface.

"Which is where I'm headed," said Boba. "Better get there, fast!"

He took a final look at the Acclamator. Then he
hit the thrusters. *Slave I* shot toward Xagobah.

Outside, streamers of purple and lavender
whipped past. Boba thought about the troopship. It
certainly looked like the Republic had sent an entire clone army to lay siege to Wat Tambor.

From what Boba knew about the Separatists,
they would have their own army, geared to fight back.

A droid army. Battle droids, super battle droids,
spider droids, the works.

Boba's grip tightened on *Slave I*'s controls. He
had successfully fought droids back on Tatooine,
when he rescued Ygabba and the other kids from
the evil Neimoidian.

But he'd never had to fight an entire army of them!

"Good thing I have my body armor," said Boba.
"And my blasters . . ."

The ship's nav program showed he was fast approaching the surface. He still wasn't sure what
Xagobah looked like, close up.

But he knew what he would find there —
Trouble.

CHAPTER SEVEN

Boba locked *Slave I* into cruising mode. Outside, shreds of dark purple mist flew by like flocks of winged mynocks. Boba watched the haze grow thicker — and darker — the closer he came to Xagobah's surface

I still have no idea what kind of life-forms are native to this place, he thought. He peered through the writhing fog. It was almost impossible to see anything, which meant it would be difficult for others to see him.

"That's a good thing, too." Boba reached for his jet pack. "The Republic is after Wat Tambor. And Wat Tambor will be busy defending himself against the clone troops — and none of them will be happy to see me coming!"

He turned back to *Slave I*'s console. Outside, the mist no longer moved. Instead, it hung like a heavy, purplish curtain over everything. As *Slave I* cruised a short distance above the surface, Boba got his first glimpse of Xagobah.

And what he saw there was disgusting!

"Mushrooms?" exclaimed Boba.

Only these weren't ordinary mushrooms. They were as tall as trees; as tall as the rock formations that surrounded Jabba's fortress. He saw orange fungi shaped like towers, with long rubbery appendages dangling from them like arms. He saw entire forests of umbrella-shaped mushrooms, yellow, crimson, poisonous green. In spots the ground was covered with a carpet of wriggling things like hair or fur. They waved and changed color as the ship passed overhead, darkening from pink to darkest violet. Some of the tallest mushrooms sported fungi like ladders crawling up their sides. Really crawling, like slugs or gigantic swollen caterpillars.

"Gross!" said Boba.

Though it was also sort of cool, in a horrible way. He stared at a huge fungi that looked like a bloated jellyfish. It pulsed and belched clouds of purple-black smoke as Boba's ship hovered above it.

Only it wasn't smoke, but spores.

"That's what the fog is," Boba realized in amazement. "Not mist, or clouds — but billions and billions of mushroom spores! I wonder if it's safe to breathe?"

Quickly he logged into the ship's medical computer and read the data there.

It is recommended that you take an antidote before setting foot on Xagobah, as a precaution. Most of the fungi are harmless, but some have toxins that can be fatal if swallowed or breathed. Others can cause changes to non-native biological entities.

"Like me?" asked Boba, as he took a small inhaler out of his med kit.

Boba breathed in the antidote, then tossed the empty inhaler.

"Changes," he mused. "I wonder what kind of changes? Well, I'll have plenty of time to find out — later. Right now I'm out to find Wat Tambor."

Slave I was cruising well below the mushroom forest's canopy now.

But in the distance, Boba could see something other than rubbery fungi and coiling tendrils.

Laser fire.

He stared out as bolts of bright blue flame erupted through the haze of purple and black. For a moment the flares illuminated the scene below.

"There it is," breathed Boba.

In the center of a large clearing an immense structure loomed: Wat Tambor's fortress. It was too dim to see clearly. But Boba could make out dark slashes about 500 meters from the citadel —

a series of trenches engineered by the Republic's troops. More laser fire rose from here, streaking toward the fortress walls. Boba could just make out myriad forms moving through the shadows.

"Clone troopers," he said aloud, preparing to land. "This is where the action is. Which means — that's exactly where I'm going!"

Back on Tatooine, one of the first things Boba had done was arrange for his ship to be completely overhauled by Mentis Qinx. At the time, Boba had no credits to pay for the work. He'd bluffed his way into it, projecting enough confident authority that he'd fooled Qinx's administrative droid.

And the bluff had paid off. Qinx had upgraded *Slave I*'s power cells. He had installed a series of camo covers that concealed new turbolasers and concussion missile launchers. He had upgraded the engineering console. He had even replaced the existing hardware grid with a larger one. Someday, that grid would accommodate more advanced stealth hardware.

Unfortunately, Qinx hadn't installed it yet.

"That'll be your next big project, Qinx," muttered Boba.

He stared up at the vast Republic assault ship hovering just beyond the planet's atmosphere. *Slave I*'s interstitial shield had worked beautifully out there, with the Republic's eyes trained on the surface of Xagobah.

But would it work here on the planet itself?

He activated all the ship's auxiliary cloaking devices and began to land.

Below, the mushroom forest swayed and tossed as *Slave I* descended. Clouds of spores drifted across the viewscreens. In the near distance, flickers of blue and gold exploded through the violet haze. He had landed behind the front lines; if he'd tried to fly directly to the citadel, both Republic and Separatist forces would've been alerted to his presence. And Boba needed both stealth and surprise if he was going to capture Wat Tambor.

More laser fire.

The Republic's forces were very close.

With a shudder, *Slave I* touched down.

"Here we are," Boba muttered. A chill crept across him, but he ignored it. Facing down fear had become second nature to him. He glanced at his father's book, stowed safely beneath the console. Not long ago, Boba would have taken it with him for good luck, and to give him confidence.

But not now. Boba had developed discipline,

and with that came confidence. And he had memorized every word of Jango's advice. Now Boba carried the memory of his father inside him, along with the knowledge of his own strength.

As for luck? Boba took a deep breath. *We make our own luck,* Jango had told him. *Caution, cunning, preparedness — that's what luck consists of.*

Oh — and a great set of weapons doesn't hurt, his father had added with a rare smile.

Thinking of Jango made Boba smile sadly.

"Well, I've got the weapons, that's for sure," he said.

He did a brisk check of his firearms, sliding a palm shooter onto one hand. With the other he checked the array of weapons on his belt.

A vibroshiv; a single CryoBan grenade that Jabba had given him as reward for an earlier success; his blasters. The Mandalorian body armor, stronger and tougher than chyrsalide hide, as supple as Boba's own skin.

Man, this feels great! he thought, flexing his arms. He checked that his Westar blasters were fully charged. *That should be enough. . . .*

He started for the hatch, then stopped. His gaze fell upon a small object resting alongside the flight console.

Ygabba's gift.

He picked it up, feeling again how heavy it was for something so small. Carefully, he opened it.

"Whoa!" His eyes widened in delight. "A holo-shroud!"

He examined it closely: compact power cell, hologram generator and projector, hologram cartridge and tuner. As he turned it, a small text doc slid out. Boba recognized Ygabba's neat handwriting.

Boba —

Bet you didn't expect this! I used Jabba's hologram recorder to scan an image for you on the hologram cartridge. Seeing that'll be your next surprise!

The bad news is you can't check it out until you actually use it — and the power cell only lasts for two minutes. So save it for when you really need it. Can't wait to hear how it all turns out!

Your friend,
Ygabba

Boba shook his head, marveling.

"Ygabba, you definitely have the best taste in presents," he said at last. He locked the holo-shroud in place on his belt. "Guess that's it . . ."

He was ready to go. For a moment he looked longingly at his jet pack. That would sure make it faster to get around.

But as he reached for the jet pack, he heard a burst of laser fire from outside. There was an answering volley, followed by an explosion.

Boba shook his head. "Too risky."

Reluctantly he left the jet pack where it was. He adjusted his helmet so it covered his face and stepped forward, opening the airlock. For one last instant, he stopped and stared back at the interior of his ship — he hoped he'd make it back here. Then he closed the airlock and opened the outer door.

A rush of warm, marshy air surrounded him, thick with the smells of rot and stagnant water. A flare of cannon fire made the towering mushrooms shake like grass in the wind. He heard distant comm static and shouting, the scream of something that was not human.

Boba smiled. "Wat Tambor, here I come!"

His hand poised above his blaster, Boba Fett took his first step onto the surface of Xagobah — and into the unknown.

CHAPTER EIGHT

Slave I had landed in a small clearing in the mushroom forest. After checking that the area was safe, Boba ran quietly until he reached the edge of the clearing. He stopped and looked back.

His ship was gone.

For a moment Boba's heart stopped. "What?"

Could the Republic forces have found him so soon?

Suddenly he remembered. Jabba's interstitial shield! He laughed hoarsely. "Guess that proves the cloaking device works!"

Boba gazed to where his ship was hidden. *I'll be back as soon as I can,* he thought. *With Wat Tambor — dead or alive!*

He touched his helmet in farewell, turned and began to make his way through the forest.

"Ugh!"

Boba swatted at a thick, slimy purple-green tendril that reached for him from an overhanging branch. The tendril recoiled like a cratsch preparing to strike. A cloud of green mist puffed out from it, and a smell like rotten meat.

Boba grimaced. "Funny, Jabba didn't mention moving, stinking mushrooms!"

He activated his helmet's filtration system. As he stepped forward his boots sank into sticky ooze.

"Ugh!" Boba groaned again.

From the air, Xagobah's fungus-covered surface had appeared solid. But now that he stood on it, or in it, Boba saw it was about as solid as mugruebe mucus. He pulled his foot up. There was a loud belching sound, as the ground beneath sucked at his boot hungrily.

Maybe leaving the jet pack behind hadn't been such a good idea. . . .

Before he could take another step, a deafening sound tore the air overhead, followed by a blinding burst of flame. Instinctively Boba flung himself back toward an umbrella-shaped fungus three times his height.

That was his first mistake.

"Hey!" Boba shouted.

The huge mushroom had a gash in its side, big enough to hold Boba. He thought he could hide there from whoever was firing. Instead, great slimy folds of fungus suddenly extended from the mushroom, like huge mynock wings. They covered him until he was wrapped in a slimy cocoon, with only his head free. Then they yanked him backward to the base of the fungus-tree. A putrid scent filled his nostrils. Boba's hands lashed out, struggling to free himself.

That was his second mistake.

The instant his fingers touched the rippling fungus, they were stuck fast. And the more he struggled, the worse it got. Within minutes, he was entirely stuck. He could feel his blaster at his waist, but he couldn't move to retrieve it. His fingertips grazed the handle of his vibroshiv, but he couldn't free it. He could scarcely breathe.

And that, unfortunately, seemed to be the point.

Because Boba could still see. And what he saw was that he was slowly, inescapably, being pulled toward the gash in the side of the great mushroom-tree.

Only it wasn't just a gash. And it wasn't a hole.

It was moving, opening wider and wider the closer he drew to it.

And suddenly Boba knew what it was —

A mouth.

CHAPTER NINE

The fungus was like some horrible hybrid of mushroom and spider. The folds enveloping Boba were like a web.

And the mouth — well, it was exactly like a mouth! Boba could smell it, the rotting scent of whatever its last meal had been. And he could see it, row upon row of crimson, razor-sharp teeth stretching deep inside the mushroom's trunk.

Now what?

He tried kicking again.

Nothing. He was completely immobilized. The fungal tree's mouth was only meters away now. Boba glared at it through his helmet. He couldn't move them, but still his hands clenched angrily.

Wait a minute . . .

Just beneath one hand he could feel the tip of something hard and smooth: his Stokhli spray stick. Boba had taken it from a Stokhli nomad who'd given him a hard time in Mos Eisley one day.

He'd stuck it on his weapons belt and, truth to tell, he'd almost forgotten about it, despite the fact that spray sticks cost a lot of credits. It was small and slender, with a stun pad at the very bottom and spray mist cartridges a few millimeters above.

Blllaaaerghhh . . .

A sound came from the fungal tree, a disgusting moan of pleasure that Boba interpreted as "dinnertime!"

"Not yet," he grunted. He clenched his hand again, his fingertips grazing the spray stick. He had no way of taking aim at the fungus, no way of adjusting the spray mist net or the electrical charge it delivered. If it backfired, Boba would find himself entangled all over again, still unable to move —

Not that it would matter!

Aaaaergghhhh!

A pale purple tongue protruded from the mushroom's slobbering mouth. Flecks of foul-smelling saliva splattered across Boba's helmet. With every ounce of strength he had, Boba focused on moving his finger toward the spray stick.

Just an iota, just the merest fraction —

And —

There was a muffled report. At Boba's side the spray stick shuddered as though it would explode — and then it did!

"Gotcha!" crowed Boba.

A shimmering mist erupted from the stick's tip. It surrounded Boba, but it did not adhere to him. Instead it fixed itself to the slimy membrane that wrapped him like a cocoon. It formed a second web, a net strong enough to hold a charging myntor.

A powerful electrical surge pulsed through the spray mist net. *Good thing I have my helmet and body armor!* Boba thought.

As the pulsing charge stunned its prey, Boba flung himself forward. Around him the fungus membrane slackened then recoiled.

He was free!

He heard an unhappy slurping sound, then a sort of sizzling groan. The next instant he was on the ground, rolling away from the mushroom tree. He stopped himself, then clambered to his feet. His hand felt for the stun stick, disabling it.

"Well, that came in handy," he said.

A few meters off, the mushroom tree quivered and moaned. The stun-net covered its mouth. Its pale tongue poked pathetically at the webbing, while above it the tree's umbrella crown drooped.

"Only a great bounty hunter could have pulled that off!" boasted Boba as he brushed himself off. "And —"

He stiffened. His hand hovered above his

blaster as he turned, as slowly as he dared, to face the creature behind him.

"And only a fool would have approached a flimmel tree during feeding hours," it said coolly.

"Who are you?" demanded Boba.

But he might have asked, *What are you?*

The creature regarded him calmly. It was reptilian, a little taller than Boba and with long, muscular arms and legs clad in what looked like a camo uniform of purple and gray. Its large, almond-shaped eyes were coldly intelligent, its lipless mouth curved in a slight smile to reveal sharp teeth. Its wiry forearms were curled around a blaster rifle.

And the blaster was pointed right at Boba Fett.

CHAPTER TEN

"Who am I?" repeated the creature. "On Xagobah, we like to ask questions before we answer them. But —"

The roaring whine of a missile passed overhead. Boba flinched. A moment later the missile impacted a short distance away, sending him falling to his knees. He looked up to see the creature staring down at him, still eerily calm.

"But we seem to find ourselves on the same side for the moment," the creature went on, as though nothing had happened. The muzzle of its blaster remained fixed on Boba as it motioned for him to get up.

"And what side is that?" snapped Boba.

"The wrong one," retorted the creature, as another missile whizzed overhead. "Quickly!"

It jammed the blaster rifle into Boba's side, gesturing toward the mushroom forest.

"No way!" Boba shook his head. "I've already made dinner plans, and they don't include being the main course!"

The creature made a low growling sound. Boba stiffened, then realized the thing was laughing. "Dinner plans!" it repeated. "That is good! Feeding time is over —" It poked him again, harder this time. Reluctantly, Boba began moving toward the fungi forest.

"The flimmel trees share an underground root system," the creature continued. "They are thousands of years old, and when one is hurt, they all suffer. And that one was very badly hurt!"

It indicated the flimmel tree that Boba had escaped from. Its canopy had retracted completely. It looked like a closed — and very mournful — umbrella.

"None of them will be hungry for a little while." The creature shot Boba an admiring glance. "That was a good jolt you gave it."

"Thanks," said Boba. He regarded the creature warily. But its own expression as it stared back at him was mostly curious. Boba positioned his hand so that it was near his blaster.

What's the best way to deal with this thing —whatever it is? he wondered.

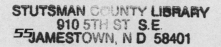

The alien was armed, but so was Boba. He could blast it — but what if there were others nearby?

He looked at the alien from the corner as his eye. As he did, the echo of laser fire made the surrounding mushroom forest shake as though a gale tore through it.

I don't even know what side of the conflict it's on, Boba brooded.

A sudden staccato burst of comm static made up his mind.

That was way too close, Boba thought. And he could tell from a glance at the alien that it felt the same way. Boba decided to take matters into his own hands. He adjusted his helmet, squaring his shoulders to make himself seem as tall as possible.

"We better find shelter — fast," he said.

To his surprise, the alien nodded. "This way," it said, turning to lope into the forest. Boba followed, trying not to trip over clumps of dimly glowing mushrooms like tiny, domed cities scattered underfoot. He kept his hand on his weapon, scanning the shadowy fungus-growth around him for signs of an ambush.

Thankfully, he saw nothing, save the clusters of gleaming mushrooms and the occasional flimmel tree. They ran for several minutes. A second burst of comm static sounded — much closer this time. Boba could even make out words: *Tambor Angalarra, Ulu, Suspect Ambush . . .*

Suspect ambush. Boba's grip on his blaster tightened. Scant meters ahead his reptilian guide paused in front of an enormous mushroom tree the color of demonsquid ink. Like the flimmel tree, it was topped by a parasol-shaped crown. Unlike the flimmel tree, this one had wobbly limbs protruding from it. They reminded Boba of the spokes of a wheel — if the spokes had started to melt.

"This way!" hissed the alien. It made a running leap and nimbly swung its clawed forearms over the lowest branch. The entire fungus seemed about to keel over. Almost immediately the plant straightened, its limbs coiling and uncoiling like fingers.

"Hurry!" the alien called urgently. "Come here!"

Boba stared up at it. Its lidless jade-green eyes stared back. Then it turned and began clambering farther up the fungus stalk. As it did it made a soft clicking sound, as though it were talking to the mushroom.

The entire tree shuddered as a low rumbling sound shook the air.

"Uh, thanks, but no thanks!" Boba yelped. He started to back away. Before he could move, the tree's lowest branch snaked toward him. It looped itself around his waist, firmly but gently; then quick as lightning pulled him into the air.

Kaflooom!

Fragments of dirt and shattered fungus pelted him. Boba stared at the ground in horror. Where he had stood, there yawned a mortar hole the size of a speeder. Flickers of flame ran around its perimeter. He smelled the ozone stink of a pulse grenade.

"That was way too close!" exclaimed Boba. Beside him the alien nodded.

"Indeed," it said.

Boba blinked. For the first time he realized where he was: halfway up a huge fungus, with an armed and possibly hungry reptile next to him. He was outnumbered, at least for the moment.

Better play dumb, he thought.

"Uh, I know you don't like to answer questions — but can you tell me exactly what's going on?"

The alien regarded him with its calm, intelligent eyes. It looked him up and down, taking in his Mandalorian body armor and helmet, his weapons. One of its clawed hands absently stroked the stalk of the fungus tree.

After a moment it spoke — but not in answer to

Boba's question. It gave a series of clicks and growls, seemingly directed to the tree. The tree responded by extending a long slender tendril toward Boba's head.

Ulp! he thought, but stood his ground. The tendril touched his helmet, then his chest. It remained there, pressed against the smooth body armor. Boba could feel his heart pounding. After a moment he realized the tree could feel it, too.

It's checking me out!

Boba felt a sneaking admiration. The alien reptile looked at Boba and nodded. Its mouth parted in a razor-toothed smile.

"The fungus has a primitive sensory system that responds to heat and motion. It detects an elevated heart rate. Your garb indicates you are a warrior and, I suspect, a mercenary one intending to attack me. I am not a warrior."

The alien leaned against the fungus stalk. Its jade eyes grew clouded. "But I have learned to bear weapons, as you see. My name is Xeran. I am a Xamster. My family has been bound to this malviltree, Malubi, for one thousand turns of Xagobah. Once hundreds of us lived here and harvested Malubi's spores. Now only I remain."

Xeran's voice grew sad. "War has come to

Xagobah. Though we wanted no part of it, still war claimed us. Many of my people have been forced to serve one side or the other. Many others fled, only to be shot in flight. Our malvil-trees are dying of neglect and loneliness. And now I am caught between two armies —" It lifted one clawed hand and pointed. "There. Can you see them?"

Boba strained, but even adjusting his helmet's focus didn't help. "No," he replied.

The alien made another series of clicks. The fungus tree — Malubi — extended another tendril. This one was thicker and less rubbery. The alien hopped onto it, then motioned for Boba to do the same. He did, and the alien grasped him as the tendril bore them up, up, up, until they were at Malubi's very top.

"Wow," breathed Boba in amazement.

Up here they were above the velvety haze of purple spores. Boba could see the canopy of the mushroom forest waving gently beneath. He could see the little clearing where he had left *Slave I*, though of course his ship was invisible to him behind its cloaking device.

And —

Boba's breath caught in his throat. He grasped tightly at Malubi's rubbery appendage. He was glad

Xeran could not see his face behind his Mandalorian helmet. Because the top of the malvil-tree also gave him a clear and terrifying view of what he had come here for.

From the air, the Republic's trenches had looked like slashes in the ground. Now Boba saw how carefully constructed they were. Each held a line of thirty or so clone troopers, heavily armed. Waves of fire erupted from the trenches, arching through the air toward the fortress. With each bombast, a group of clone troopers would charge from the trenches —

Only to be met by an opposing charge of droids!

Boba whistled. The Republic's forces were impressive — he figured there were hundreds, maybe a thousand, clone troopers arrayed on the battle field below. But the citadel was so well-defended that Boba could not suppress a gasp.

"Jabba was right about Wat Tambor," he muttered. *A master of defense technologies*, the gangster had said of him; and now Boba could see how true that was. Through the haze of spores and laser fire, Boba got his first glimpse of the Separatist's droid army: lines of battle droids marching relentlessly, tirelessly, toward the clone troopers to breach the Republic's lines.

That looked bad enough. But what made Boba's hand tighten on his blaster wasn't the clashing armies.

For the first time, he could clearly see Wat Tambor's citadel.

CHAPTER ELEVEN

"So that's it," murmured Boba.

"Yes," said Xeran. "The Mazariyan Citadel. The cause of all my troubles."

"And the beginning of mine," Boba replied, trying not to shiver.

Mazariyan rose from the planet's surface, unimaginably immense, a looming dull black. Its sides were stepped, like the sides of an ancient pyramid of Yavin. But even from this distance Boba could tell that the edifice was not just a building.

The dull black, smooth surface seemed to pulse with life. Flickers of energylike lightning ran up and down its sides. On the levels above, shining black spines protruded. The spines were twice the length of Boba's body and as sharp as javelins. He could see where dark shapes had been impaled upon them. Even as he watched, one of the spines began to slowly retract, like a machine. Boba watched in horror as a limp form slid from it, falling and bouncing down the fortress's side.

"The tyrant who is holed up there has twisted the evolution of Xagobah's life-forms," said Xeran. His tone was steady, but Boba saw that the alien's face was strained. "He has taken fungus that were benign, feeding only on bacteria. He has taken our gentle malvil-trees. He has bio-engineered them so that they are now perverted and kill things without feeding on them."

"Things like humanoids," said Boba in a low voice.

"That is correct," agreed Xeran. "And Xamsters."

"What is this tyrant's name?" asked Boba.

But he already knew what the answer would be.

"Wat Tambor," said Xeran. "He is evil. And as you can see, he has brought evil to us —"

Xeran pointed to where a dark mass stretched about five hundred meters from the citadel in its long shadow. "Those are just some of the Republic's troops gathered there. They have laid siege for weeks now. No matter how many arrive, few are able to gain entrance. And when they do, we hear rumor of what they find inside. Wat Tambor's command of technology has made him ruthless. There are no prisoners inside his citadel. And no survivors."

Boba looked back at Mazariyan. He found he could not take his eyes from the sight, horrible as it was. "The Republic's using clone troopers," he said, more to himself than Xeran.

"Yes. Sometimes the Republic has forced my people to fight, paying them well. Yet the Republic has lost many non-clone fighters. Fighters they could not afford to lose. So their chiefs have sent in a Jedi General named Glynn-Beti to lead their forces."

Boba's eyes grew cold and hard. "Glynn-Beti?"

He didn't speak his thought: *She's the Jedi who Jabba told me about.*

"Yes. Glynn-Beti is a Jedi Master, and a fearless warrior. Also a shrewd one."

"She can't be that shrewd," said Boba. He smiled coldly. "Otherwise her troops would have already captured Wat Tambor and taken the citadel."

To Boba's surprise, the reptilian alien once more made the growling sound that passed for Xamster laughter.

"That is very amusing!" Xeran's jade-green eyes fixed on Boba. "It is a rare gift, to be able to find amusement when faced with danger. Or death."

He peered at Boba more closely. "You have not told me your name, stranger, or your business here. And I will not ask you. I suspect we share a common enemy. And if that is the case, it is best I do not know your intent. That way I cannot betray you."

Boba nodded. "Thank you," he said.

"Though I can, perhaps, help you." Xeran glanced at Boba's weapons belt. "You are already well-armed. Better armed than I am," he said, and patted his own blaster. "My weapon came from a trooper I was forced to slay in self-defense. He would have harmed Malubi."

The Xamster stroked the malvil tree. "No, stranger. I do not think I can offer you better weapons. But I can offer you advice.

"All of this territory is disputed, with battles erupting at anytime." Xeran pointed to the battle-field below them. "Your only hope of approaching the citadel is to come down from the north — that is the far side, there."

Boba's heart sank. "There are a thousand clone troopers between here and there!" He patted his blaster, then shook his head. "But I have no other choice, so —"He started to climb down.

"Wait." Xeran's cool scaly hand gently restrained him. "You may not have a choice. But you do have a means of approaching without being seen."

The Xamster turned. Standing on tiptoe, he extended his claws to pluck a dark purple globe from the malvil-tree's stalk. As he did, a small puff of violet smoke emerged from the globe, then disappeared. Once more Boba felt the malvil-tree tremble, then grow still.

"This globe contains Malubi's spores," explained Xeran. "The spores are harmless in themselves. Yet they are not useless. They act as a powerful camouflage agent. Organic life-forms cannot see through the haze produced by the spores. Neither can the droids — the spores reflect light too high on the spectrum for the droids to register through their optics. Wat Tambor has exploited the spores for his own purposes, to camouflage his vessels. But when the spores are carried by the wind, they act as chemical messengers between the trees."

Xeran's lipless mouth curved in a smile to reveal white razorlike teeth. He held up a small pouch, opened it, and took a pinch of what looked like lavender powder between his claws.

"Here," he said, gesturing at Boba's hand. "Take this. Put it into your eyes, beneath your helmet. It will enable you to see through the haze."

Boba held out his gloved hand. Xeran dropped a small amount of the lavender powder into his palm. Boba stared at it, then at the Xamster.

Could Xeran be trusted?

Boba hesitated. He had learned over the last few years to trust his instincts — one of a bounty hunter's most powerful assets.

And his instincts told him now that Xeran was telling the truth.

"Thanks," Boba said. He turned away, momentarily raising his helmet. He tilted his head back, and let a few grains of the powder fall into his eyes. He felt a faint prickling, but that was all. He blinked, lowered his helmet, and turned back to Xeran.

The Xamster nodded approvingly. "The effect is not permanent. But it may help you. And here —"

He held out a small purple orb. "Take this globe with you. Malubi has already imprinted you as one who means us no harm. The other malvil-trees will recognize you. They will not harm you. But if you have need of camouflage, crush this globe. The spores will be released."

Boba took the globe. "Thank you," he said. Carefully he slipped it into his utility pouch.

"Something else I will tell you," added Xeran. "There is a fungus we call Xabar. It has many small tentacles. It is a very deep purple in color, with brilliant red tips. Wat Tambor has taken this fungus as well and made it into a weapon. Its tentacles release a toxin. The toxin causes paralysis. Not permanent, fortunately. But very effective. Anyone who comes into contact with it is immobilized. Completely. Consciousness remains, but not the ability to move."

"Thank you," said Boba. "I will remember."

From somewhere beneath them came a burst of laser fire.

"I have to go now," said Boba. He looked down at the battlefield that stretched between him and Wat Tambor's living citadel. Then he turned to Xeran. "I owe you one, Xeran. Thanks again."

The Xamster nodded solemnly. Its jade-green eyes narrowed, and it smiled. "You do not need to thank me. When you destroy our shared enemy, do so in the memory of my malvil. That will be thanks enough for me. And for Malubi," he added.

Boba smiled. As he did, one of the malvil-tree's tentacle branches snaked around him. Very gently it lifted Boba, then slowly brought him to the ground.

"I will not forget!" Boba called back as Xeran waved at him. "For Malubi!"

"For Malubi!" Xeran echoed.

Lifting one clawed hand in farewell, the alien slipped back into the violet shadows of his malvil-tree.

CHAPTER TWELVE

A hundred meters up in Malubi's violet canopy, Xagobah had for a little while seemed a quiet, even peaceful, place.

That peace was shattered as soon as Boba's feet touched the ground.

"Captain! Intruder in your sector!" a voice shouted from only a few meters off.

His father's voice.

For an instant Boba froze. Then brilliant blue flame exploded, close enough that he could feel its heat through his body armor.

"Whoa!"

With a muffled shout Boba dove for the under-brush.

The voice shouted again. "Captain! Did we score a hit?"

Boba crouched beneath an overhanging net of webbed fungi. He peered out and saw a figure stalking into the clearing.

His father's figure, cloaked in the gleaming, gray-white body armor and mask of the Republic army.

A clone trooper.

"Captain, do you copy?"

Boba tried not to breathe as the trooper moved with sure, heavy steps, until he was just an arm's length from where Boba was hidden. He was close enough that Boba could clearly see the back of his helmet.

Boba had seen the clones many times before, of course. He could remember them being raised by the thousands on Kamino. And he had met a young clone, 9779, on Aargau. Clones were known mainly by their numerical designation.

Could this be 9779, grown to his full size?

The thought made Boba feel slightly sick. He forced it from his mind, and stared from the shadows at the trooper. Like all the clones, the captain had his father's build. It also had Jango's strength. Boba could tell from how easily it hefted its weapon, a DC-15 rifle that would have made Boba's arm ache.

"Checking it out," the clone answered into its comlink. "I see no sign of an intruder. Hold your fire."

It gave one more look around the clearing. Then it slid its rifle back into an upright position, turned, and strode off.

"Whew." Boba let his breath out in relief. That was close!

He waited until the clone trooper was just a pale fleck among the mushroom trees. Then Boba began to follow it. He kept within the shadows of the overhanging fungus, moving swiftly and stealthily as a stalking cratsch.

Now and then a slender mushroom stalk would reach out tentatively to brush against his helmet, or touch his hand. Whenever this happened Boba would pause, holding his breath.

But it seemed as though Malubi's spores must have warned the other fungus of Boba's coming. Their tendrils would only touch him. Then they would withdraw. Sometimes a small puff of purple would appear above him. Then he would see other mushroom trees ahead of him swaying gently.

Thanks, Xeran, Boba thought. *And Malubi.*

He patted the trunk of a very young malvil-tree, then stopped.

In front of him, the mushroom forest abruptly ended. Beyond it, the ground looked scorched. When he looked up he saw the hovering shadows of Republic ships, like black clouds in the purple mist. When he looked down, he saw black circles where transport vehicles had landed and departed. In other places, there were holes and small craters left by exploding weaponry. Smoking bits of vegetation were elsewhere. And other things, too. Things Boba wished he hadn't seen.

For reassurance he made sure the purple globe was still in his pocket. His hand tightened on his blaster.

He waited, trying to figure out what to do next. There was no point running out into the middle of a battle. *Nine-tenths of any bounty hunter's success is proper planning,* Jango had always told him.

"So all I need is a plan," Boba muttered.

He squinted through the haze of smoke and spores. From here he had a clearer view of Wat Tambor's citadel.

It sure didn't look any better. It was well-guarded, for one thing. In addition to the gigantic black spines that protruded from the fortress, there were droids patrolling its perimeter.

Battle droids, Boba noted grimly. He counted thirty — not enough to fight a war, but more than enough to keep intruders at bay.

There were other droids, too. Crablike defense droids swarmed around a triangular opening that seemed to be Mazariyan's entrance. He saw several hulking modified super battle droids and mounted laser towers.

And, hovering above the peak of Wat Tambor's

fortress, a great, dark, shapeless mass. It was like a purplish-black thunderhead or a huge amoeba, floating over the battlefield.

"What's that?" Boba adjusted the focus on his helmet, then blinked, feeling a faint prickling behind his eyes as the form above him took on more solid outlines.

Xeran's spores were working. Suddenly he could see clearly. And what he saw was that the massive shape was not a cloud.

It was a fleet of Separatist fighters, cloaked by the spore-haze. As Boba watched, one of the droid-commanded fighters fired upon the Republic's assault lines. A spurt of flame exploded from one of the trenches.

A direct hit!

Boba steadied himself as the impact shuddered through the ground like an earthquake. He looked up again, and this time could make out something else — a darker, misshapen silhouette that hung directly above the citadel's peak. Droids swarmed around it, loading it. With a shock, Boba suddenly realized what the huge shadowy object was.

A ramship.

Boba shook his head in dismayed disbelief. Robot ramships were manufactured in the most notorious reaches of the Outer Rim. They were designed and outfitted by criminal techs —

But wasn't that exactly what Wat Tambor was?

A ramship had no organic crew. It used the hull of an abandoned — probably stolen — warship, with enough firepower to destroy a huge starship in a single explosion. The entire vessel was nothing but a massive bomb, piloted by a kamikaze robotic drone with no goal except destruction.

In this case, the Republic's destruction.

Boba craned his head back. His eyes tried to pierce the violet haze of Xagobah's atmosphere.

Somewhere up there was a Republic troopship. And while Boba had no love for the Republic, at the moment, they shared a common enemy.

Wat Tambor.

And that ramship was Wat Tambor's vessel.

The enemy of my enemy is my friend, Jango had once told his son. Boba had been too young then to understand those words. They sounded like a puzzle.

A puzzle he had just solved.

He saw clone troopers just within the borders of the mushroom forest. The Jedi General Glynn-Beti would be there somewhere, acting as commander. Presumably there were other Jedi as well, fighting as part of the Republic forces.

But he didn't see any life-forms, human or alien, defending Mazariyan. No Xamsters; no humans. Not even any mercenaries from lawless places like Carratos or Ord Mantell.

Only droids.

He's going to have that ramship smash into the Republic troopship! Boba sucked in his breath with excitement. *Wat Tambor thinks that will end the siege — and it will!*

Boba looked around furtively, thinking fast.

If Wat Tambor's vast flying bomb struck the troopship, it would destroy the Republic's chances of capturing the dangerous Separatist.

It would also destroy Boba's chances of capturing Wat Tambor.

Which meant it would destroy Boba's future as Jabba's favorite bounty hunter!

Can't have that happen! Boba thought.

But what if the ramship could somehow be commandeered into destroying Wat Tambor's citadel — and with it, Wat Tambor?

Two can play this game, thought Boba. He crouched in the shadows at the edge of the mushroom forest. He stared up at Mazariyan.

Two can play this game — but only one can win. And that one will be — me!

CHAPTER THIRTEEN

So now he had a plan. All he needed was a way to use it.

My jet pack's no good, he thought with regret. *Not enough strength or speed to go up against a ramship. Gotta try to find a vehicle . . . a speeder would be nice . . .* Boba scanned the area surrounding Wat Tambor's fortress. He knew that Mazariyan was well-guarded by drolds.

But Wat Tambor was not a droid. And surely not all of his guards or accomplices were droids. They would have used some form of transport to get here. . . .

"Yeah," Boba whispered. "And that's exactly what I need."

He started to run along the edges of the forest. He kept a close eye on Mazariyan, but saw nothing he could steal — er, use.

But as he circled closer to the area behind the fortress, things began to look more promising. The

Republic seemed to have concentrated its forces near the citadel's entrance. This back area was void of siege trenches. There were crates and cartons of supplies here, along with piles of twisted metal and plasteel. He saw demo droids and wrecker droids, a load-lifter piling big boxes near an opening. A single security drone appeared to be monitoring them. But it was an older model, and seemed to be busy scanning the area closest to the citadel's main entrance.

This must be a freight entrance back here, thought Boba. He hesitated and looked for signs of hidden Republic forces, but saw none. He might be able to dodge the security drone and clear the freight entrance.

I could try to get in that way. But what would I do once I actually got inside?

He hadn't worked out that part of his plan — yet.

Later, he thought. Quickly he turned and continued to circle the fortress, searching.

And then he saw it — he almost stepped on it! Camouflaged with torn mushroom fronds and malvil-limbs, it was so rusty and battered that it blended right in.

A swoop bike.

Boba looked around the mushroom forest furtively. But if there were clone troopers nearby, they were being even more stealthy than he was: He saw no one. He looked up.

And yes, the ramship was still there, like a volcanic cloud hanging above Mazariyan. The droids loading it were obviously close enough to see through the haze. Boba glanced back at the worker droids on the ground. The security drone was gone — it must have continued on its own circuit of the fortress.

And those other droids were all labor units. None of them would be programmed for surveillance or security.

"It's now or never," Boba muttered. He paused beside the swoop bike, looking over his shoulder. Then he shoved aside the dried-up mushrooms and jumped on. "And I say — now."

For one heart-stopping moment, he thought it wouldn't start. Then it sputtered and coughed. Finally, with a low buzzing sound it lurched forward.

Someone's modified it so that any sound is muffled, Boba noted approvingly. He leaned over the controls and pulled up on the throttle. The swoop shot up through the malvil-trees. Not as fast as Boba would have liked — whoever did the modifications obviously preferred stealth over speed.

Maybe they know something I don't, he thought,

and looked around. The worker droids were still laboring mindlessly by the freight entrance. Boba adjusted his helmet, increasing the focus until he could just glimpse the front of the citadel. Nothing new there, either. Above the citadel's peak, the ramship hovered in place. Boba swung his swoop around, then brought it up to full throttle. Fungus fronds lashed at his helmet as he flew up, up. When he hovered just below the canopy of the forest, he turned the swoop and started to cruise in a careful circuit.

Might as well do a little recon of my own, he thought. *That clone trooper came from someplace.*

But where?

In a minute he had his answer. Not too distant from Wat Tambor's citadel, something moved.

Something big — something really big!

A Republic All Terrain-Tactical Enforcer!

"Man, they mean business," muttered Boba. That AT-TE would be loaded with more clone troopers — dozens of them—not to mention some serious firepower.

There was no way he could commandeer an AT-TE, of course. But where there were incoming clone troopers, there would be Jedi nearby to command them. They would have vehicles of their own — gunships, starfighters, maybe even airspeeders.

If I can get my hands on an airspeeder, I might be able to decoy that ramship back toward Mazariyan. The ramship doesn't move very fast — but in a speeder, I could! Then I could reach Slave I *and get out of here — back to Jabba to claim my bounty!*

He angled closer to the AT-TE, being careful to stay out of sight. There were several smaller vehicles accompanying the walker — and, in the distance, more AT-TEs.

That's more like it, Boba thought with grim satisfaction.

Things might not be so bleak for the Republic, after all. He adjusted the long-range focus on his helmet, until he could make out even more shadowy shapes far behind the approaching AT-TEs. Gunships, each carrying a payload of still more troops and walkers.

And, sure enough, there were speeders, too — and a starfighter.

"That'll be Glynn-Beti," said Boba. He scowled, but brought the swoop down lower to get a better look. As he did, something flashed past him —

Another swoop!

"Huh?" For a second, Boba was too startled to do anything. Then he grabbed his blaster.

But whoever was on the swoop wasn't intent on catching Boba. He was heading for the citadel.

But not just the citadel. As Boba watched in amazement, he realized that he wasn't the only one who'd been coming up with a plan.

The swoop was flying up — straight toward Wat Tambor's ramship!

CHAPTER FOURTEEN

"Great minds think alike!" Ygabba used to tell Boba, joking.

But right now, watching the other swoop flying at the ramship, Boba thought maybe this particular idea hadn't been such a great one. The swoop looked like a squir-mite attacking a sandcrawler.

"He's doomed," Boba groaned.

He'd had only a glimpse of the person flying it. But a glimpse was all he needed to recognize him.

Ulu Ulix!

Boba had met the young alien back on the *Candaserri*. Of course, Ulu hadn't known Boba by his real name — Boba had called himself Teff, and had said he was an orphan from Raxus Prime. He'd guessed Ulu was about the same age as he was, though Ulu had horns and three eyes. They'd been friendly — well, as friendly as Boba could be to anyone back on the *Candaserri*.

He'd never recognize me now, Boba thought with

pride. *Not with my Mandalorian helmet on, and my body armor.*

As Boba watched Ulu's swoop approach the ramship, he remembered the other thing about the three-eyed alien.

Ulu Ulix was a Padawan, a Jedi apprentice — and his Jedi Master was Glynn-Beti!

Quickly Boba looked back to where the AT-TE was moving in the forest. A starfighter kept pace with it, high above the tops of violet malvil-trees. If Glynn-Beti was in that fighter, she must suspect the ramship was headed for the Republic's assault ship. But did she know her Padawan was headed for the ramship?

Boba wondered if Glynn-Beti was crazy — or if Ulu was.

He didn't get to wonder long.

KA-FLOOOSHH!

Meters from where Boba's swoop hovered, a malvil-tree exploded. There was a second flash of blue flame. Boba was spattered with purple gunk.

He wiped fungus goo from his helmet, yanked on the throttle, and swerved away from the forest. He needed a better view of what was happening.

What he saw wasn't good, at least not for the Padawan. The sentry droids had spotted Ulu Ulix!

Boba's swoop shuddered as another burst of flame struck a giant mushroom not far off.

BLAM!

The mushroom exploded. Fiery blobs of fungus flew everywhere, setting other trees aflame. The droids were firing! Boba's swoop shot straight up, safely out of range. He was close to the citadel now — too close, probably — but the droids weren't firing on Boba.

At least, not yet. Boba frowned. What — who — were they after? He risked bringing his swoop down lower, and nearer to the fortress. From here he had a clear view of the droids below, laser fire criss-crossing the air as the Republic's troops began to counterattack.

But the droids weren't firing on the Republic troops.

Their target was Ulu Ulix.

Boba swerved abruptly as a blast tore the air just meters away. When he looked back, he saw the ramship give a sudden surge upward.

"They've released the ramship!" he exclaimed, just as the other swoop suddenly shot toward the massive vessel. Boba waited for a volley of fire from the ramship to destroy the swoop.

But the ramship didn't alter its swift course one

meter. Instead it sped upward, oblivious to Ulu Ulix pursuing it.

And why should that surprise Boba? The ramship had a drone-mind. Nothing could cause it to alter its course. Attempting to lure or attack it had obviously been a really, really bad idea.

That could have been me, Boba thought.

He watched grimly as Ulu's swoop dipped and swerved clumsily. The alien was trying to avoid the barrage of fire from below. But his swoop didn't seem to have any more thrust than Boba's.

"Still, he *could* fly it better," Boba said.

He clung tightly to his swoop, flying it closer still to the citadel's black peak, and glanced back into the forest.

The convoy of AT-TEs had stopped at the very edge of the clearing. The speeders were gone, and the starfighter. Boba's jaw clenched.

Glynn-Beti doesn't even care that her Padawan is under fire. She's too concerned that her own attempt to attack Wat Tambor's citadel will be affected!

Typical Jedi arrogance, thought Boba angrily. He looked out to where Ulu Ulix's swoop swung dizzily around the top of Mazariyan. With a sudden *BOOM*, the three-eyed alien's vehicle was engulfed in black smoke. Sparks flew from it. There was a terrified cry.

And Boba watched in horror as a small figure tumbled into the air — and plummeted straight toward the waiting spines of Mazariyan!

CHAPTER FIFTEEN

Boba had no time to think. He yanked back on the throttle. At the same time he opened the stop to feed it as much fuel as possible. With a garbled roar, the swoop shot forward. Laser fire and explosions rocked the air around Boba. Below him, the spines waited.

"Master . . . help . . . !"

A cry echoed above the sound of laser fire. Boba leaned forward as far as he could, arms outstretched. His swoop raced toward the shining black pinnacle of Mazariyan. One huge, curved spine thrust upward. It positioned itself to impale the small form falling like a stone.

Boba's swoop dipped as he reached out. With a groan, something heavy crashed onto the front of the swoop. Boba swerved away from Mazariyan.

"Th-thanks!" Ulu Ulix blinked. He kept a tight hold on the swoop's fuel tank. His three large eyes stared gratefully at Boba. "I thought I was dead back there!"

"Well, there's still a chance you might be!" Boba shouted over the thunder of crossfire. "Keep your head low —"

BLAM!

Laser fire ripped past them. Boba wrestled his blaster from his belt. He turned and fired in the general direction of the sentry droids. Then he glanced down. Battle droids were everywhere now. Some were still firing up at Boba. But most had bigger targets in their sights.

With a deafening rumble, the first of the AT-TEs had drawn up at the edge of the clearing. Its hold opened, and a wide gangway swung down. More than a dozen clone troopers came running out, blasters firing. There was the whoosh and roar of battle droids rushing from hidden entrances in the citadel. They marched in formation toward the Republic's troops. Bolts of pure energy zoomed toward the clones. Wat Tambor's fortress glowed like the sun as laser fire rippled up and down its sides.

Ulu Ulix's three eyes widened as he stared at the carnage below.

"Wow," he breathed.

The attack on Mazariyan had begun.

"Keep your head down!" Boba commanded. He abruptly swung the swoop to the left.

A blinding burst of energy exploded behind them. Boba cut back on the throttle. The swoop dropped sickeningly before he pulled it out of the dive.

He yelled, "We've got to get out of here, fast!"

"There!" gasped Ulu. He pointed to where another AT-TE waited. It was surrounded by a squad of heavily armed clone sentries. "General Glynn-Beti!"

Boba squinted through the thick smoke. "Where?"

"She's standing by the transport — see? She should be in her speeder, keeping track of the battle. I guess she was worried about me. Boy, she looks really, really mad."

Ulu Ulix gulped. Boba looked at him. He couldn't help grinning inside his helmet. "Mad?"

"Yeah . . . the siege was ready to begin, anyway, but . . ."

The three-eyed alien looked back to where his swoop lay. It was now a heap of smoldering wreckage. It was surrounded by battle droids who were busy firing on the Republic's troops.

"But maybe the siege started a little earlier than scheduled?" Boba finished Ulu's sentence for him.

The alien nodded miserably. "Yeah. Something like that."

Boba steered the swoop to where Glynn-Beti stood. He glanced at Ulu Ulix. It was weird to think that the horned alien didn't recognize him in his helmet and body armor. Weird, but good.

I was more of a kid back then, Boba thought proudly. *But now I'm a real bounty hunter.*

The swoop approached the edge of the forest. The sentries guarding the AT-TE snapped to attention. They stared up at Boba. They raised their weapons. They were ready to fire —

"Get Glynn-Beti's attention!" Boba shouted at Ulu Ulix over the roar of battle. "Otherwise we're dead!"

"Master!" yelled Ulu. "Master, here — !"

On the ground, Master Glynn-Beti looked up. She was small and slender, with a vaguely feline face crowned by flowing reddish hair. Even from this distance, Boba could sense the power she held.

A Jedi's power.

CHAPTER SIXTEEN

"Ulu Ulix!" The Jedi's voice rang out sharply over the din. She sounded angry, but also relieved. She turned to the clone sentries. "Hold your fire!"

Boba angled the swoop down to within a few meters of the AT-TE. It landed with a bump. Ulu clambered off. He smoothed the folds of his Padawan's robe. Then he looked at Boba.

"I don't know how to thank you," said the three-horned alien. "I don't even know your name. Although there *is* something familiar about you. . . ."

Ulu frowned slightly, thinking. Boba said nothing. He felt light-years older than Ulu. Light-years older than he had been when they first met.

Fortunately he didn't need to say anything. Because General Glynn-Beti was bustling toward them now. And she looked like she had plenty to say.

"Ulu! What were you thinking?" She glared at the young alien. Ulu Ulix stared at his feet, abashed. "You put this entire mission in jeopardy!"

"I am sincerely sorry, Master," Ulu said. "I am ashamed of my actions. But I only wanted to help."

"Help?" Glynn-Beti scowled at him. Then she looked at Boba, still on his swoop. "This stranger is the one who helped!" The Jedi bowed slightly. "I am in your debt, stranger. My profound thanks for saving the life of this most foolish of Padawans."

Boba nodded. "You're welcome." He was uncomfortably aware of Glynn-Beti's keen gaze boring into him. But an instant later her attention was elsewhere.

"Trooper!" she commanded. "You may all resume your watch! As for you —" She turned to Ulu Ulix. "You will remain by my side for the rest of this maneuver. Unless you prefer to wait on board the troopship?"

Ulu Ulix shook his head swiftly. "No, Master! I will obey this time."

"Good." Glynn-Beti began to walk away. But she had only taken a few steps when she stopped. She turned and stared at Boba.

Uh-oh, he thought.

"What is your place in this battle, stranger?" she asked. Her voice was calm, but there was a threat hidden in it. "You are not part of my battalion. And you are obviously not working for our enemy. You have not come from *there* —" She tilted her head at the citadel of Mazariyan. When she turned back to Boba her gaze was piercing. "We have sent some of our most valued soldiers inside — ARC troopers. They seldom fail us. Not one has returned from that place. Have you?"

Boba hesitated. The Jedi might be able to detect a lie. If she did, she could take him prisoner, whether or not he had saved her Padawan. At worst, he might languish in a Republic cell. At best, she could send him off-planet, back to Tatooine — where he would face the rage of Jabba the Hutt.

A prison cell might be preferable to that.

Boba stared back at Glynn-Beti. He was very glad she could not see his face behind his helmet.

"No. My sympathy lies with the Xamsters," he said.

The Jedi seemed to mull this over. Finally she nodded. "Very well. I will not detain you. The natives of Xagobah are in dire need of whatever help they are given." She beckoned Ulu Ulix to her side. "Come. We have much to do."

"But Master —" Ulu stopped. He gazed up at a dark blur in the violet haze of Xagobah's atmosphere. "What about the ramship?"

"We are well aware of the ramship, Ulu. Someone more experienced — and wiser — than you will deal with it."

Ouch! thought Boba. *Wonder who that might be?*

He watched as the Jedi and her Padawan headed back toward the AT-TE.

Just before they boarded the AT-TE, Glynn-Beti turned and shouted back to Boba, "Yes. Someone else will take care of the ramship. You, stranger, might want to launch your solitary attack at that moment. Mind my words!" The Jedi Master then disappeared from view.

Boba quickly powered up his borrowed swoop. It gave a hoarse cough and sputtered into the air.

Boba circled back to where the siege was in full swing. The air blazed blue and black and silver with laser fire. Everywhere around the fortress, clone troopers were attacking Wat Tambor's droid forces. *What did the Jedi mean?* he wondered.

It looked like the Republic was in trouble.

The Separatists had launched a counterattack!

"This isn't good," Boba muttered. "Not for me, at least!"

Boba had thought that Wat Tambor's citadel was well-guarded before. Now he realized the canny Separatist had deliberately hidden the full power of his forces. Because suddenly the gaping maw of Mazariyan yawned open. There was a horrible, thunderous clattering sound, and hundreds — maybe thousands — of droids came streaming from the fortress. Spider droids, super battle droids, even dreaded and lethal droidekas, like gigantic insects rolling out of a rotten stump.

Boba gaze down at them, transfixed. "How am I going to get through that and into the fortress? There's no way I can land without being seen and pulverized!"

He steered the swoop down for a closer look. Too close.

With a grinding noise, one of the droideikas came to an abrupt halt. It swiveled and uncurled into firing position, its black, eyeless head pointed straight up — directly at Boba.

It fired.

"Aghhh!"

Too late, Boba yanked at the swoop's controls. A blast of heat struck the swoop. At the same instant, Boba dove from it. He could feel the surge of fire through his protective boots. He could hear the concussive blast roaring through the air like a seismic charge.

But all he could see was the explosion of laser fire all around him as he plummeted helplessly — right into the battle.

CHAPTER SEVENTEEN

"Ummmpph!" With a grunt Boba smashed onto the ground. His body armor absorbed the blow, but it took him a moment to catch his breath. There was such a thick haze of smoke and spores he could barely see. He blinked, trying to clear his vision.

What he was able to make out was not good: a clone trooper, just millimeters from his face!

"No way!" yelled Boba. He rolled onto his back and kicked out, just as the clone took aim. Boba's feet connected with the clone's knees. He wasn't strong enough to knock down the trooper. But Boba did throw him off balance.

And that was all it took. Boba was on his feet again, blaster raised. The clone towered above him, its face invisible behind its helmet. But something in the way it stood, something in the way it held its blaster, made Boba hesitate.

Because, just for a flickering moment, it wasn't a clone trooper there.

It was Jango Fett — Boba's father.

Boba recognized Jango's stance. He recognized Jango's strength. He even recognized the way Jango's head drew back slightly as he aimed his weapon. Only this wasn't Jango Fett. This was a clone trooper who had decided that Boba was an enemy.

"You're not my father!" Boba's voice was drowned in the blast from his Westar. "You're a clone!"

The trooper's aim was excellent — but Boba's was better. In a blaze of flame and vapor, the clone trooper fell.

One down! thought Boba. *Only a couple thousand to go.*

He whirled, and found himself smack in the middle of the battle about 200 meters from the citadel walls. Above him, droid fighters shot from the citadel's peak. Battle droids swarmed around its base, blasting away. Clone troopers ran in formation. As they neared the fortress, the formation broke up. Individual troopers raced toward the battle droids. One clone got caught by a hailfire missile and vanished into a thousand pieces.

Yuck! thought Boba. He looked away quickly.

BARRAAAMMM!

Brilliant multicolored pulses of laser fire erupted from the clones' blaster rifles. All were now aimed at the rolling, firing hailfire.

KRRRAARRROW!

A direct hit! One of the hailfire's wheels disengaged and the clone's body was dragged into the ground by the still churning second wheel. A few moments later it exploded in a fiery blast.

But the Republic's troops were still in danger. They were vastly outnumbered, for starters. And somewhere above them, the ramship was headed for their assault ship.

That was bad enough. But what was worse — the droidekas were laying waste to the clones. They rolled across the battlefield, safe within their shimmering forcefields. Laser fire bounced from them harmlessly. Harmless for the droidekas, anyway. Some of the pulses ricocheted back and mowed down the very troopers who had fired them.

With a cry Boba dodged a sudden flare of blue. A super battle droid stalked toward him, took aim and —

BLAAM!

Boba fired. The upper half of the droid disintegrated into shards of flaming plasteel. Boba whirled and blasted another droid. It fell. Boba staggered backward, struggling for breath.

I can't keep up with them, he thought desperately. *There's too many! The droids are fighting the clone troopers. The troopers are fighting the droids —*

And they're all firing at me!

Around him was chaos. Black smoke mingled with clouds of purple spores from malvil-trees and giant mushrooms caught in the crossfire. Boba adjusted his helmet, striving to see through the haze. Xeran's powder is wearing off, he thought with dismay. *The Republic's getting wasted.* Not that he cared about the Republic. But if Wat Tambor was powerful enough to destroy them, what chance did Boba have?

Plenty, Boba thought grimly. *I'm not giving up.*

A sudden roar made him look up. For a split second, every battle droid paused. As though they shared one mind, they all looked up, too.

"Starfighters!" cried Boba.

A phalanx of starfighters arrowed through the haze. Wat Tambor's air defenses fired at them in a blaze of blinding energy. The starfighters' leader banked sharply to the right. Boba stared up at it, admiringly.

"He sure knows what he's doing." He thought of Ulu Ulix, and smiled. Then he adjusted his helmet's focus as he took cover behind a wrecked vehicle. "Let's get a better look at this guy . . ."

But now the battle droids had also seen the fighter. A barrage of ground fire shot up toward it. The starfighter dove. Pulses exploded in the empty air as the ship raced downward through the flak generated by the citadel's air defenses. It made a lightning pass at the heads of the droids, decapitating dozens as it flew incredibly low. It was so close to the ground that Boba could see who was piloting it.

"Skywalker!" Boba felt a spike of excitement. He had seen Anakin Skywalker from a distance in the arena of Geonosis. The young Padawan was older now, but Boba recognized Anakin's defiant gaze — and his skill. "He can really fly that thing!"

Anakin's starfighter pulled up once more. A blaze of Separatist fire sparked around it. Then, without hesitating, the ship went into another dive. It came in low, pulling up at the last moment as it lobbed an energy charge at the citadel.

KARRROOOM!

The charge exploded. Flaming spikes of durasteel flew everywhere. A raw smoldering hole appeared in the citadel's side.

"Yes!" said Boba.

Wish I could do that! Boba thought as another spasm of flame arced by him. Boba jumped, then ran through a throng of clones. He was now using all the skills he'd acquired as a bounty hunter. His blaster fired without pause. Droids exploded in orange sparks — and clones fell left and right, as he fought his way toward the fortress.

This time, Boba didn't feel bad at all.

CHAPTER EIGHTEEN

Near the foot of Wat Tambor's citadel, a homing spider droid had fallen. Its large form slumped over on two of its legs, forming a small, protected area.

Boba headed for this makeshift refuge. He had to leap over several dead clones, and the smoking wreckage of a swoop. But once in the shadow of the droid he was safe. For a few moments, anyway.

Now what?

Boba crouched, panting, and stared out at the battlefield. The clone trooper reinforcements were holding their own against the Separatists, but were unable to advance. Boba doubted they'd be able to defeat Wat Tambor's forces. The clones were organic and could be killed. And they *were* being killed in great numbers. The droids couldn't regenerate, but there seemed to be an endless supply of them streaming from the citadel's mouth.

But could it really be endless? Surely even Wat Tambor's army had a limit?

Boba peered out from the crook of the fallen droid's elbow. Far above him, Anakin Skywalker's starfighter led the Jedi forces in the air attack. They were targeting the spider droids.

As Boba watched, he saw another hailfire come spinning out of the shadows of the malvil-trees. It rolled toward the center of the battlefield, scattering clones like leaves. It stopped. It raised its missile launcher, taking aim at one of the starfighters. With a deafening burst of energy, a barrage of plasma pulses went soaring upward — directly toward Anakin Skywalker's yellow starfighter.

He's doomed! thought Boba.

But the Padawan had other plans. Just as the plasma bursts approached it, he arrowed his starfighter to one side. The energy bolts continued onward, up, up, up through Xagobah's violet sky —

And found another target — the ramship!

"Whoa!" Boba whooped.

An immense starburst of pure energy like a thunderbolt surged out from where the ramship had been. Boba tensed, waiting for fallout; but none came. The energy stored in the ramship was so dense and powerful that the explosion caused it to self-implode.

Score one for the Republic!

Quickly, Boba scrambled between the fallen spider droid's legs. He stared out at the battlefield. For a moment, everything had come to a standstill. Battle droids and clones alike gazed up at the waves of energy rippling through Xagobah's atmosphere — violet, scarlet, gold.

"Very pretty," muttered Boba. He glanced at the entrance to Mazariyan. He couldn't believe it.

No droids were there!

Boba looked around again. And yes, battle droids and sentry droids alike all seemed distracted. This was the moment Glynn-Beti had foretold!

It's the energy surge! Boba realized. *It's momentarily scrambled their command centers.*

This was his chance!

Staying as low as he could, Boba darted from the shelter of the spider droid. He raced toward the fortress, breathing hard. The entry to Mazariyan gaped, faintly gleaming. Just a few more meters and he was there. None of the clone troopers would make it in time; they were still too far off.

Boba paused, hand on his blaster. Behind him, the sounds of battle began once more. In front of him was a problem: The maw of Wat Tambor's citadel opened onto the Separatist's stronghold — and blades of purple fungus ringed the entrance like razor teeth. Rows of spines stuck out threateningly, ready to pierce any intruder. He recalled what Xeran had told him and suddenly Boba understood.

Wat Tambor had perverted Xagobah's fungus to his own ends — inside his citadel.

I have to get in there, Boba thought desperately. *But how?*

Boba shoved his blaster into his belt. He drew his vibroshiv.

No, he thought, and reluctantly replaced it. *That will just make it worse.*

Boba's hand moved from his belt. That was when he felt something in his pocket. Something round.

And suddenly Boba remembered.

Xeran's spore-globe.

What was it Xeran had said?

"If you have need of camoflage, crush this."

Boba pulled the globe from his pocket. He stared at the purple sphere in the palm of his hand.

It looked harmless. And Xeran had said it was harmless — to Boba. But he had also said the spores acted as chemical messengers. Could they somehow damage the citadel?

Well, here goes nothing!

Boba glared up at the massive structure. Then he raised his hand, and, hoping this wasn't a mistake, he crushed the globe.

It was like the energy surge that had destroyed the ramship. Only this surge was darkest purple and smelled faintly of spices.

And it was, somehow, sentient. Boba watched in awe as a vast spore-cloud enveloped the base of the fortress. The cloud moved like a gigantic paramecium. And as it did, the spines nearest to Boba drooped. As Boba stared, fascinated, he saw more metallic spines struggling to emerge.

But for the moment the spore-cloud was stronger. The spines withered. New ones wriggled helplessly, then seemed to melt away. But more kept coming, needle-sharp, and Boba quickly realized that the spores were just a temporary solution. And whatever camoflage they offered would be temporary, too.

Now! he thought, and turned back to the entrance. Sure enough, the rows of spines had withered. They hung in limp black ribbons around the opening. Boba lunged forward, head down. Around him the spore-cloud was already starting to disperse.

If I can just get inside . . .

Tiny spines began to poke through the entryway. Tiny razor-sharp petals thrust from the edges of the opening. Boba grabbed his vibroshiv and slashed at them. Then, with one last desperate lunge, he leaped forward. Metallic strands of fungus slashed at his helmet. Writhing silvery vines slithered from the entryway —

Too late!

With a gasp, Boba's feet connected with the ground. He staggered forward into a murky purplish tunnel, heedless of the spikes behind him. Beneath his boots the floor trembled like kallil-virus jelly. From the curved durasteel walls, pale silvery fronds and stems waved like dead fingers. There was a smell of scorched metal — and a faint, ceaseless *thrum* as if some unimaginably vast machine heart was beating somewhere out of sight.

Boba took a deep breath. Then, with every bit of courage he could command, he stepped forward —

Into the citadel of Wat Tambor.

CHAPTER NINETEEN

It took several minutes for Boba's eyes to adjust to the dimness.

Yet it was not completely dark. An eerie greenish haze hung over everything. Glowing orbs appeared to be set into the fortress's curved, metallic walls. When Boba drew close to one, he saw that it was not an orb, but a mushroom — a luminous mushroom. Wat Tambor had bioengeneered the fungus to merge with metal and plasteel circuitry. Phosphorescent bacteria made it gleam. When Boba touched it, glowing pale green slime stuck to his glove.

"Ugh." Hastily Boba wiped it off. He didn't want to be any more noticeable than he already was!

He began walking down the hallway. The walls were smooth and metallic and curved, as was the ceiling. They were covered by a film of squishy, violet fungus that squelched beneath his feet. But there were other things in the walls, too. Blinking chips and miniature monitors, shining crimson threads of circuitry like blood vessels.

Wat Tambor's genius had not been content with changing the malvil-trees' genetic code. He had developed all kinds of nanotechnology. This had enabled him to fuse computer intelligence into the fungus citadel as well.

Yet the monitors did not seem to be alert to Boba's presence. He stopped in front of one, holding his breath: nothing.

The power surge from the ramship blast must have scrambled their circuits, he thought. But that won't last long . . . better hurry!

Boba moved as quickly and stealthily as he could. He watched for droids but saw none. Now and then another curving passage would join the central tunnel. Boba peered down these.

What he saw made him content to stay in the main passage. The walls in those tunnels had strange, lumpy shapes in them. Shapes that sometimes moved or kicked or flailed. Boba wasn't certain what they were.

But he had a pretty good idea — he remembered the last ARC troopers Glynn-Beti had spoken of.

And Xeran's people — the Xamsters who had struggled against the evil Separatist. Boba gritted his teeth. He thought of the gentle malvil-trees. He thought of the gentle Xeran, forced to take up arms against Wat Tambor. Boba's hatred of Wat Tambor grew. *I will show no mercy,* he thought fiercely. *Xeran's people can no longer avenge themselves. I will take vengeance for them!*

And, of course, I'll get Jabba's bounty, too.

The passage began to climb slowly upward. As it did, it curved, as though Boba were climbing some gigantic spiral staircase. He passed shimmering walls where monitors flickered yellow and green and red. He passed a room like the hollow chamber of a human heart, pulsing slowly in and out. He passed tube-shaped openings that gave him a fragmented view of the battle below.

But he passed no droids. He passed no clones. As far as Boba could tell, he was the only thing that walked inside of Mazariyan.

And that made him nervous.

Could Wat Tambor have left? Could he have somehow escaped before Boba arrived here to capture him?

Boba frowned. *I sure hope not.*

Things had been bad enough outside, with the citadel under siege. He suspected they could get much worse if he was found inside by Wat Tambor's troops — or the Republic's.

He continued his journey, in and up. The air

grew thick and heavy. Boba made sure his helmet's intake filter was working. He thought of the violet haze of spores that surrounded this planet. He could only imagine what kind of disgusting, protective spores were produced inside Mazariyan.

Sometimes an unpleasant thought would work its way through Boba like a splinter.

What if I never find him? What if I can't find my way out?

He was working on pure intuition now. The curved passage seemed to spiral endlessly up into the fortress. Sometimes it would branch. When that happened, Boba would choose one way or another, on instinct.

He came to another place where the tunnel divided. To his left, it curved upward, its smooth walls gleaming purple. To Boba's right, the passage curved slightly downward. Here the tunnel had a deeper glow, almost indigo.

Wonder what that means? thought Boba.

For a moment he paused, thinking. Then he placed his hand on his blaster, and walked boldly into the right-hand passage.

He hoped he'd made the right choice.

Up until now he had — but not anymore.

Boba didn't know it yet. But his good fortune was about to dissipate like the malvil's spores.

CHAPTER TWENTY

The air here was warmer; so deep and dark a blue it was almost black. Boba didn't want to risk shining a light in the tunnel. He adjusted the infrared on his helmet, but that seemed to make it worse. So he moved very slowly, feeling his way. His gloved hands stuck to the slick walls. The soft, dank floor sucked at his boots. Worse, the faint thrumming sound was louder here. He could feel the floor vibrating under his feet. Ahead of him, the tunnel's walls grew uneven. As Boba drew closer, he quickly yanked his hand away.

Flabby, pale, fingerlike growths extended from the wall's surface. As Boba stared, they wriggled like the tendrils of a Bestine sea anemone. The tendrils were dark purple. Their tips were crimson.

"The Xabar fungus!" Boba exclaimed, recoiling. He remembered Xeran's warning: The tentacles released a paralyzing toxin.

"Who goessss there?"

A hissing voice slashed through the air. Boba looked up sharply.

"Stranger — identify yourself!"

Boba felt his stomach clench — but not with fear. Anger had been building inside him ever since he entered the fortress.

Now it boiled over.

A shadowy figure stood before him. Tall, with greenish skin, cold deep-set eyes, a lipless mouth. Even in the indigo darkness Boba recognized him.

The Clawdite, Nuri!

It had been two years since Boba had last seen him. That was on Aargau. The shapeshifter had been smaller then. So had Boba.

But Boba was definitely bigger now — bigger, and stronger, and heavily armed. And this Clawdite had betrayed Boba. Boba had trusted him. In return, the shapeshifter had stolen what remained of his father's fortune.

"Nuri," Boba said in a low, controlled voice. He saw the Clawdite's eyes narrow. "You owe me."

"Owe you?" The Clawdite did not recognize him. His gaze shifted uncertainly from Boba to the passage behind him.

"That's right," said Boba. He drew his vibroshiv.

He lunged for the shapeshifter. As he did, Nuri's form seemed to melt. His neck grew longer and longer. His arms and legs shrank into nothingness. His head narrowed. Long, knife-sharp teeth filled his mouth. Feathered scales covered his body. Where the Clawdite had been, a huge arrak snake drew back to strike. Its glittering green eyes fixed on Boba. Then, hissing furiously, it wrapped its coils around him.

"Not so fast!" Boba yelled. He struggled against the thick, powerful serpentine shape. The arrak snake's coils began to tighten. Boba fought for breath. His vibroshiv fought to discover some weak spot in the snake's scaly armor —

And found it! Just beneath the snake's fanged jaw there was a patch of flesh unprotected by scales. Boba plunged the vibroshiv there — when once again the shapeshifter's form changed!

In place of the arrak snake was a copper-colored dinko. It had crushing jaws, and pointed talons the length of Boba's arm. Its jaws snapped at Boba. When he kicked back at it, a foul-smelling spray squirted from the dinko.

"Ugh!" Boba staggered backward. For a moment even his Mandalorian helmet was no help — the fumes choked him. Then his secondary filters kicked in. Coughing and shaking, Boba struck back. The dinko snarled, lashing at him with one long, pointed talon. Boba's hand fumbled for his

blaster. He grabbed the weapon and was just raising it to fire, when the dinko abruptly faded.

Going, going . . . gone.

"Hey —!"

Boba blinked, trying to find whatever the
shapeshifter had become. And saw a giant fefze
beetle, the same color as the walls. It crawled
through the toxic Xabar fungus. Then it scuttled into
the shadows.

"No!" Boba shouted and lunged after the es-
caping insect. But he could barely see it in the
darkness. Desperately he took aim with his blaster.

No, wait — Boba shook his head. *That's what he
wants! If I fire, I'll alert everyone in the fortress —
assuming there's someone here!*

He shoved his weapon back onto his belt. He
could just make out the beetle skittering down the
tunnel. Boba took a step back, then took a running
leap. As he flew through the air he leaned forward,
keeping the black shape in sight.

Uuumph!

With a grunt Boba fell. The slimy floor beneath
him shuddered. His hand grasped at darkness for
the beetle —

And got it!

"You're not going anywhere!"

This time Boba kept a firm hold on the slick

scales. Moments later he was grappling with the full-grown Clawdite.

"Don't forget, I have this," Boba hissed. His vibroshiv suddenly hovered inches above Nuri's neck. He felt the shapeshifter slump in defeat.

"That's better." Boba stared coldly at Nuri. The Clawdite glared back at him. "Now — I need an answer. Fast. Where is Wat Tambor?"

Nuri bared his teeth. "I don't know what you're talking about."

Boba drew the vibroshiv to within a hairbreadth of Nuri's flesh. "Do you want to feel how much closer this can get?" he whispered menacingly. "I know who you are, Nuri. I know you helped the Techno Union spring Wat Tambor from prison. Now I want to know — where is he?"

The Clawdite hissed. Its evil eyes glittered. It stared at Boba's vibroshiv. Then it drew a long shuddering breath.

"That way —" Nuri's head twitched, indicating the passage leading down. "The central chamber. He's there."

"Is he well-guarded?"

Nuri's eyes fixed on Boba. The vibroshiv hummed above the Clawdite's neck.

"No," said the shapeshifter reluctantly. "He sent the last of his droid forces to join battle with the Republic. But Grievous is coming — and he will bring reinforcements."

"Grievous?" Boba frowned. "Who's that?"

"The General." The Clawdite stared at him with hatred. A slow, nasty smile spread across his face. "Whoever you are, I can see that you are working alone. The Republic will not come to your aid. You will meet General Grievous soon enough, stranger — and when you do, he will destroy you!"

CHAPTER TWENTY-ONE

Boba snarled in rage. "Those were your last words, Clawdite!"

He began to press the vibroshiv against the shapeshifter's jugular vein. Then he stopped.

If Nuri's body is found, Wat Tambor will know there's an intruder inside his fortress. But if I let him go, he'll sound the alert. . . .

Boba looked around the dim tunnel. His gaze lit on a clump of the paralyzing Xabar fungus.

That's it!

He began to drag the Clawdite toward the fungus. Nuri fought furiously. But Boba was stronger.

"I've been really curious about how this stuff works," he said. He pinned the Clawdite to the ground, then grabbed the shapeshifter's arm. "Now I can find out."

Nuri struggled as Boba pushed his arm down.

Sensing prey, the Xabar's tentacles reached upward, wriggling in anticipation.

Closer . . . closer . . .

The Clawdite's hand hung above fungus. Then, like pale, grasping fingers, the tentacles grabbed him.

"Unnnhhh . . . !"

Abruptly the Clawdite went slack. He hung, dead weight, from Boba's hands. Boba recoiled, worried that the toxin might somehow reach him.

"Nuri?" he said in a low voice. "Nuri?"

The Clawdite sprawled before him. He looked dead. He had no pulse. He was not breathing. His eyes stared upward, blank and cold as stone. When Boba gingerly touched his arm, it felt stiff.

"Well," Boba said, scrambling back to his feet. He gazed at the fallen Clawdite lying beside the Xabar fungus. If anyone found him, they would assume he had accidentally stumbled upon the paralyzing mushroom. "I hope that stuff works for a good long time. Long enough to get me to Wat Tambor, at least."

He began to run down the passage. It was noticeably warmer here. And there were more signs of Wat Tambor's technological genius.

Ribbons of circuitry gleamed along the tunnel's soft, slimy walls. Phosphorescent globes hung alongside shining plasteel tubes that crackled with electricity. Computer monitors the size of Boba's thumb blinked like crimson eyes. Xabar fungus sprouted from discarded bits of droids like hair.

And always there was that steady, powerful thrumming, like the beating of a massive heart.

Boba tried not to think about that too much. He didn't like to imagine what kind of creature would have a heart that size.

Ahead of him the deep-blue glow of the tunnel began to brighten. Now it was hard to see the walls of the passage behind all the layers of metal and computer circuitry. The tunnel turned, and turned again. Boba's steps slowed. He crept alongside the wall, eyes fixed on what was before him.

Just a few meters away, the tunnel ended. A high, smooth archway opened into a single large chamber. Silvery violet light spilled from it, threaded with deep purple and blood red.

The light was so intense it hurt Boba's eyes. He paused and adjusted his optical sensors. Then he checked his weapons. His blasters, his vibroshiv, Ygabba's holoshroud, ion stunner, dart shooter . . .

Which would help him capture Wat Tambor?

All of them — or none?

Boba's stomach clenched. For the first time a shiver of apprehension went through him.

Fear is energy, he told himself. *Use it.*

He took a deep breath. Then, keeping as low as he could, he ran the last few meters from the tunnel through the archway.

And found himself face-to-face with Wat Tambor.

CHAPTER TWENTY-TWO

Boba sucked in his breath sharply.

He was in a large chamber, more like a cavern than a room. Blinking and shimmering circuits covered the slivery walls. Banks of monitors stretched everywhere. There were heaps of parts belonging to droids — arms, legs, blasters, power cells. Clumps of Xabar fungus sprang up between them, and other mushrooms as well.

None of this surprised Boba.

But what was in the center of the chamber did.

Thrusting up from the floor was a huge, shapeless, purple mass. It pulsed and shuddered like a massive slime mold. Flickers of crimson flame raced inside it. From it protruded dozens of tentacle-like tubes. Each time it pulsed, Boba could see darkly glowing violet liquid stream through the tubes, feeding outward into the walls.

There were other veins as well. These rippled from the walls and into the bioengineered nerve center, feeding it. The liquid that surged through them was deep red.

Boba stared at it, revolted. This was why none of Glynn-Beti's ARC troopers returned. He was gazing at Mazariyan's heart! That was how the *enormous* fungus received its power — by feeding on what it found *inside*!

A deep voice shattered Boba's thoughts.

"You are not who I was expecting."

Boba looked up. In the center of the room towered the Separatist. His own expression was momentarily as surprised as Boba's.

Wat Tambor was tall and powerfully built. His body was encased in combat armor that he had designed himself. Only the top of his ridged skull was visible above it. His eyes were hidden behind round optic sensors. A heavy metal cowl covered his mouth and the lower part of his face.

When Wat Tambor spoke, his inhuman voice was calm. "So. An intruder. That is no matter. I will make use of you — one way or another!"

He raised his hand. A ray of scarlet light surged from it. With a cry Boba dove to one side. The ray struck the floor, pulverizing plasteel into smoking goo.

Wat Tambor cursed. Boba rolled, drawing his blaster. He fired.

BLAM!

The blast from his weapon arced straight toward Wat Tambor!

Boba's joy abruptly died. Tambor was quicker than he looked, and dodged the blast, which was then seemingly absorbed by the chamber wall.

Boba felt the entire room around him shudder. The huge nerve center gave a powerful surge. The shimmering circuits glowed even brighter.

"Your weapons only serve to feed it," announced Wat Tambor in that calm, mechanical voice. "As you will yourself!"

Boba staggered to his feet again. "No!" he shouted.

Mazariyan's tentacles were everywhere. Writhing, wriggling, crawling along the floor — dozens of them, with a single target.

Boba Fett!

With a cry Boba drew his vibroshiv. He slashed at a huge vein and felt his blade cut into it with a satisfying slurp. Shimmering liquid splattered out. He ducked to one side, nearly falling on the slick floor.

But the chamber floor was already at work, sucking up the liquid greedily.

"Take that!" cried Boba. A cobralike tentacle swooped toward him and he grabbed it. It lashed up, scraping the ceiling. Boba hung on with all his strength. He waited until he was just above where Wat Tambor stood beside Mazariyan's beating nerve center. Then he let go.

"Yaaah!" he shouted.

He lunged for the Techno Union Foreman, blaster firing.

Too late. Wat Tambor moved too quickly.

The Separatist whirled, sending another bolt of energy flying from his hand. Boba lunged for the floor. If he could just reach that pile of broken metal . . .

"Agh!"

A blazing burst of pain struck his leg, so powerful it overwhelmed his body armor, which now cracked and smoked. Boba crashed against the ground. He had a glimpse of Wat Tambor's figure searching for him. Then the Separatist suddenly looked away, toward the chamber's entrance.

I've got to hide, thought Boba in desperation, *before he sees I'm down. . . .*

He rolled and began to drag himself to the heap of droid parts. It was darker there. He might be able to gain a minute, enough time to get Wat Tambor in his sights once more.

Boba drew himself up by the wall. The shattered droids gave him enough shadow to hide, for a moment. In the middle of the room the tentacles were still gulping eagerly at the fluid leaking from the severed vein.

"Where is he?" Boba murmured. He rubbed his leg. The pain was subsiding — it had only been a glancing blow. "Gotta find him —"

Boba strained to see Wat Tambor. But the Techno Union Foreman was out of sight, hidden by the bulk of the nerve center.

Boba could hear him, though. He was talking to someone — but who? Nuri?

I should have killed the Clawdite! Boba thought angrily. *Now he's betrayed me again!* He began to ease himself from the shadows. One hand remained firmly on his blaster. The other was on his belt, ready to draw whatever weapon he might need.

But as Boba looked up, he realized he'd be needing all of them. Because into the room strode the most terrible, vicious figure he had ever witnessed.

Its head nearly touched the ceiling — a head composed of interlocking bands of an alloy he'd never seen before. A pale, cowled robe cloaked its body. Through its folds Boba glimpsed its true form: gleaming metallic limbs, six-fingered hands like robotic claws. When it turned its head, searching, Boba saw its eyes. Golden reptilian eyes, the pupil a black slash set within blood-colored sockets. Even Mazariyan's tentacles seemed to sense his awful threat. They retracted into the heart, like a carnivorous snail into its shell, waiting.

Boba's blood froze. Suddenly, and with horrible certainty, he knew he was looking upon the most powerful, most lethal threat he had ever faced.

The terrifying general of the droid army — Grievous!

CHAPTER TWENTY-THREE

Boba's mouth went dry. Grievous was flanked by two droid bodyguards, nearly as tall as he was. Their eyes were huge and round and crimson. They scanned the room methodically, heads sweeping back and forth.

Any moment they would find Boba!

Now what? he thought. His hands moved quickly over his weapons belt. The blasters' energy would just feed Mazariyan. And his vibroshiv would be useless against a droid.

Suddenly his hand felt something else. A small compact object, fitted neatly on his belt.

Ygabba's holoshroud.

Yes! Boba moved so that he was sitting upright. He peered out.

Grievous's bodyguards had started circling the room, scanning for the intruder. Grievous stood ominously in the center of the chamber by the heart, waiting. Wat Tambor was near a monitor, busily inputting information.

Grievous hasn't seen me yet, Boba thought. *He doesn't know exactly what I look like, or who I am.*

Boba had no idea what image Ygabba had scanned into the holoshroud. But it was this or nothing.

This is my best chance for living long enough to thank you, Ygabba, thought Boba. *It better be good!*

His finger hovered above the holoshroud's button. He took a deep breath. Then he pressed it, and stood.

There was a hum from where the cell hung at Boba's waist. Then he was surrounded by a glowing halo. It extended high above his head. When he moved his arm, the halo moved. When he stepped forward, it moved too.

From inside the holoshroud, Boba could see only this shimmering cloud. But others, he knew, saw something completely different. They saw whatever image Ygabba had scanned into the cell.

But what image was that?

As Boba stepped forward, the droid bodyguards snapped upright. Their empty, glowing eyes burned even brighter. Boba moved to one side, heading for the arch that led out. As he did, he caught a glimpse of his reflection in a monitor screen. At the same time, the bodyguards spoke.

"Durge!"

Boba almost yelped with joy.

His friend had scanned Durge's image into the holoshroud!

And that was what the droids saw: not Boba Fett, but the hulking figure of one of the galaxy's most feared bounty hunters!

"Destroy him!"

An icy commanding voice thundered through the chamber. Grievous pointed at his bodyguards. As one, they lunged forward, firing. Boba leaped aside, and the blasts struck the wall behind him. It exploded in shards of plasteel and oozing fungus. One of Mazariyan's tentacles poked out from the pulsing heart of the citadel. Grievous turned and raised a hand threateningly. The tentacle shrank back.

"I said, destroy him!"

The droids stalked across the room. Boba fired back at them. His blasts bounced off their armored forms. He yanked out his ion stunner and fired. A surge of ionic plasma flared from it. One of the droids fell back, momentarily stunned.

"Yes!" crowed Boba.

He could see his own reflection mirrored in viewscreens across the chamber, tall and powerful. For an instant it seemed that the bodyguards might be taken aback as well.

"It is indeed Durge," one said in its cold robotic voice.

Grievous turned his horrible eyes upon Wat Tambor. "You said it was a Mandalorian warrior," he said.

Wat Tambor looked at him. "He must have brought reinforcements," he replied.

"It is no matter," said Grievous.

Boba sent another bolt flying from the ion stunner at the bodyguards. Then he turned and started racing for the door.

The holoshroud's illusion would last for only two minutes. How much time was left? Enough to make the bodyguards hesitate before attacking him again?

Everything around him was a glowing blur as he ran for the arch. If he could only escape from this chamber, he could hide within the citadel. He already had a plan for utilizing those tentacles to capture Wat Tambor. If only he could —

Vvvvvvmmmmmm . . .

The hum from the holoshroud's power cell suddenly grew silent. Around Boba, the veil of Durge's image flickered into pixels of color. For a second he could see himself clearly, as the others had seen him: not Boba but Durge, his mighty arm raised to fire, Boba's weapon shrouded in the image of Durge's own blaster.

Then the holoshroud's illusion was gone. The power cell had run out.

And so had Boba's luck.

CHAPTER TWENTY-FOUR

"That is him! The intruder!"

Wat Tambor's voice rang out like a clear bell. Boba watched as Grievous and his two bodyguards turned to stare at him.

"You are not Durge, as I suspected." Grievous's voice was cold, with no trace of human emotion. "But you will die all the same!"

He lifted his arm. Before Boba could move, Grievous gave a command. A blinding flash of energy leaped from an unseen weapon held by one of his bodyguards. It struck Boba in the chest and he fell, another piece of his father's armor smoking and cracked.

"Get him," commanded Grievous.

The droid bodyguards sprang forward. But Boba's body armor had absorbed the blow's impact. He rolled to one side, struggling to his feet and backing against the wall.

"You won't take me!" he yelled.

"Maybe not alive," said Wat Tambor calmly. "But dead will suit us just as well."

The droids stalked toward Boba. He grasped a blaster in each of his hands and raised them. He waited until the droids were just meters from him. Then, ducking, he fired and darted to one side.

KABLOWWW!

The blasts bounced harmlessly from the droids. They swiveled, firing in staccato bursts. Boba fired back.

KABLAAM!

He inched along the wall, blasters flaming. *If I can just reach the door,* he thought desperately.

There was another blast of power from the droids. Right above Boba's head the wall fragmented. He took advantage of the cloud of splintered metal and mushroom ooze, and ran.

Beside him fresher, cooler air streamed from the dimness — the tunnel. Boba made for it, his breath coming in short, deep bursts as he ran. He could hear the clack of the droids' measured footsteps behind him. He could imagine their arms raised, and that terrible, cloaked figure watching —

Don't think! Move!

He dove for the entrance. Cool air embraced him, and blessed darkness. His feet touched the now-familiar, slimy surface. Before him stretched the passage. Just up ahead it divided.

If I can make that fork, I can lose them, Boba thought. His heart strained as he raced toward it. *If I can just —*

Searing pain tore through him.

Boba cried out in agony.

He struggled a few steps more.

Another torturous stab penetrated his armor from behind.

He fell.

"So," an icy voice echoed through the tunnel "Now I see you as you truly are."

On the ground, Boba writhed, trying to reach his blaster and turning to look behind him. Above him the cloaked figure of General Grievous loomed into view — and in one hand it now gripped a lightsaber glowing in the haze.

How could this be? Was the general a Jedi?!

Grievous's eyes were yellow orbs within a skeletal, silvery mask. Behind him stood Wat Tambor, flanked by the droid bodyguards.

"Not that it matters," the icy voice continued. Grievous's other hand slid from the folds of his cape and then emerged with a second lightsaber ignited. "Because you are going to die now."

Boba struggled vainly to reach his weapons

belt. Pain lanced through him, as though flames ran through his veins. He fell back.

"It looks as though he is in death convulsions already," said Wat Tambor.

And suddenly Boba had an idea. Without turning his head, he let his gaze flicker across the floor of the tunnel. There, not a millimeter away, a pale clump of the paralyzing Xabar fungus sprouted.

Can't — be — seen — moving! Boba thought. His hand crept toward the fungus. *Must — reach it!*

Grievous drew back both lightsabers to strike. Boba tensed. He let his hand rest upon the ground. He moved his wrist, fractionally, so that his glove slipped upward.

A tiny patch of his skin was now exposed.

"He's dead," Wat Tambor repeated. "Our troops await us outside, General."

The young bounty hunter held his breath. From the corner of his eye, he could see fingers of faintly glowing fungus. They were so close that he could almost feel them — almost touch them —

Now!

Something cool and damp licked the patch of exposed skin upon his wrist. His hand, and then his wrist, grew numb. A freezing breath seemed to exhale into his lungs.

"General," urged Wat Tambor.

The icy numbness spread through Boba's body. He tried to breathe but could not. He felt his heart pump feebly. His vision began to dim. His mission to capture Wat Tambor had failed.

What would his father have thought?

Xeran said the paralysis was only temporary, Boba recalled as he drifted off. *He better be right. . . .*

Around him the chamber began to grow even more dim. A flicker of consciousness raced through Boba's brain. He recalled how Jabba would sometimes have his prisoners brought to him, frozen in carbonite.

Wonder if it feels like this . . .

It was the last thing Boba thought.

"General, please!" said Wat Tambor. "Look at him — he's dead. No one could have survived those blows!"

Wat Tambor came up to him and nudged at Boba's senseless form. The bounty hunter's body moved, but did not respond. Grievous swept past the Techno Union Foreman, in turn. Disengaging the lightsabers, he kicked Boba.

"Dead," echoed one of the droid bodyguards.

"Dead," the other repeated.

"Leave him," said Wat Tambor. "There will be plenty of time to dispose of the body when we return. And plenty of others to join him, too," he added with a malicious mechanical laugh.

"Come!" commanded Grievous. "He is no Jedi. I will not waste my skill any longer on such a lackey." He turned, then stalked down the passage, Wat Tambor at his heels. The bodyguards followed, the citadel echoing as they passed. In the tunnel, a dark form remained, motionless, senseless, upon the ground.

Outside, the siege of Mazariyan raged on.

Inside, Boba Fett's battle for life was just beginning.

CLONE WARS
TIMELINE

With the Battle of Geonosis (EP II), the Republic is plunged into an emerging, galaxy-wide conflict. On one side, the Confederacy of Independent Systems (the Separatists), led by the charismatic Count Dooku and backed by a number of powerful guilds and trade organizations and their droid armies.

On the other side, the Republic loyalists and their newly-created clone army, led by the Jedi. It is a war fought on a thousand fronts, with heroism and sacrifices on both sides. Below is a partial list of some of the important events of the Clone Wars and a guide to where these events are chronicled.

MONTHS (after *Attack of the Clones*)

0　　**THE BATTLE OF GEONOSIS**
Star Wars: Episode II – *Attack of the Clones* (LFL, May '02)

0　　**THE SEARCH FOR COUNT DOOKU**
Boba Fett #1: *The Fight to Survive* (SB, April '02)

+1　　**THE BATTLE OF RAXUS PRIME**
Boba Fett #2: *Crossfire* (SB, November '02)

+1　　**THE DARK REAPER PROJECT**
The Clone Wars (LEC, May '02)

+1.5　　**CONSPIRACY ON AARGAU**
Boba Fett #3: *Maze of Deception* (SB, April '03)

+2　　**THE BATTLE OF KAMINO**
Clone Wars I: *The Defense of Kamino* (DH, June '03)

+2　　**DURGE VS. BOBA FETT**
Boba Fett #4: *Hunted* (SB, October '03)

+2.5　　**THE DEFENSE OF NABOO**
Clone Wars II: *Victories and Sacrifices* (DH, September '03)

CLONE WARS
TIMELINE [continued]

MONTHS (after *Attack of the Clones*)

+6   **THE DEVARON RUSE**
Clone Wars IV: Target Jedi (DH, May '04)

+6   **THE HARUUN KAL CRISIS**
Shatterpoint (DR, June '03)

+6   **ASSASSINATION ON NULL**
Legacy of the Jedi #1 (SB, August '03)

+12   **THE BIO-DROID THREAT**
The Cestus Deception (DR, June '04)

+15   **THE BATTLE OF JABIIM**
Clone Wars III: Last Stand on Jabiim (DH, February '04)

+24   **THE CASUALTIES OF DRONGAR**
MedStar Duology: *Battle Surgeons* (DR, July '04)
Jedi Healer (DR, October '04)

+30   **THE PRAESITLYN CONQUEST**
Jedi Trial (DR, November '04)

+31   **THE XAGOBAH CITADEL**
Boba Fett #5: *A New Threat* (SB, April '04)

KEY:

DH = *Dark Horse Comics, graphic novels*
www.darkhorse.com
DR = *Del Rey, hard cover & paperback books*
www.delreydigital.com
LEC = *LucasArts Games, games for XBox, Game Cube,*
PS2, & PC platforms www.lucasarts.com
LFL = *Lucasfilm Ltd., motion pictures* www.starwars.com
SB = *Scholastic Books, juvenile fiction* www.scholastic.com/starwars